There was this mirror. A flyspecked full-length mirror that swivelled in a frame. I looked at myself. I thought I'd look different but I didn't so I stuck my tongue out. 'Just look at you,' I sneered. 'You're so *good*, aren't you, Jacqueline Hyde? So yuckily, sickmakingly good. See how *clean* you've kept yourself, even in this mucky old attic. Grandma *will* be pleased.'

I hated my reflection. *Hated* it. I know it sounds daft but I did. There was a flatiron on the floor. A rusty flatiron. I bent down and grabbed it and snarled, 'Here, Jacqueline Good – catch.' I got that mirror dead-centre and it shattered, spraying glittering fragments everywhere . . .

Also available by Robert Swindells, and
published by Doubleday/Corgi Yearling:

Jacqueline Hyde

ROBERT SWINDELLS

ILLUSTRATED BY ANGELO RINALDI

CORGI YEARLING BOOKS

JACQUELINE HYDE
A CORGI YEARLING BOOK : 0 440 86329 5

First published in Great Britain by Doubleday,
a division of Transworld Publishers

PRINTED HISTORY
Doubleday edition published 1996
Corgi Yearling edition published 1997

5 7 9 10 8 6 4

Copyright © Robert Swindells, 1996
Illustrations copyright © Angelo Rinaldi, 1996

The right of Robert Swindells to be identified as the author of this
work has been asserted in accordance with the Copyright, Designs
and Patents Act 1988

Corgi Yearling Books are published by Transworld Publishers,
61–63 Uxbridge Road, London W5 5SA,
a division of The Random House Group Ltd,
in Australia by Random House Australia (Pty) Ltd,
20 Alfred Street, Milsons Point, Sydney, NSW 2061, Australia,
in New Zealand by Random House New Zealand Ltd,
18 Poland Road, Glenfield, Auckland 10, New Zealand
and in South Africa by Random House (Pty) Ltd,
Endulini, 5a Jubilee Road, Parktown 2193, South Africa.

Printed and bound in Great Britain by
Cox & Wyman Ltd, Reading, Berkshire.

For Jennifer Luithlen – Special Agent

'My devil had long been caged, he came out roaring'
from *The Strange Case of Dr Jekyll and Mr Hyde*
Robert Louis Stevenson (1886)

Hi. I'm Jacqueline Hyde, and I know what you're thinking. You're thinking two things. One, Jacqueline's a bit of a mouthful; I bet she gets Jackie. And two, that name's familiar somehow. Jacqueline Hyde. It reminds me of something.

I'm gonna leave you to think about number two, and you're dead wrong on number one. I *never* get Jackie. I'm not a Jackie. Jackie sounds sort of tomboyish and it doesn't go with my image. My *good girl* image. You know the type. Always polite. Never late. Keeps her clothes and shoes clean. Always gets to give out the books at school and help visitors on Parents' Evening. The sort of kid who gets adults saying, Oooh, isn't she *good*. Sugar and spice and all things nice. In other words I'm the sort of kid who makes other kids want to throw up.

Perhaps I should say I was. I *was* that sort of kid, till . . . well, look – I'm going to tell you about this crazy stuff that happened to me after I found the mysterious old bottle in Grandma's attic. I don't suppose you'll believe me, and quite honestly I don't give a toss. The *old* Jacqueline would have. Oh, yes. The old Jacqueline used to burst into tears if an adult so much as suggested she might not be telling the truth. Anyway, I'm going to tell it exactly as it happened and you can please yourself.

I was at Grandma's because it was October break and the schools were shut. If schools stayed open all the time, Mum and Dad would make me go, even on Christmas Day. I'd probably have to hang up my flipping *stocking* at school if they had their way.

Well, it's the shop, see? They've got this shop that sells office machines. I won't go on about it because it's dead boring, but the point is, they spend every minute they can at the shop, and when they're not *in* it, they're talking *about* it. They never talk about *me*, and they don't listen when *I* talk. I haven't got any sisters or brothers – I don't suppose Mum and Dad could spare the time to make any – but that shop's like a favourite child. It gets all their attention. It's like a big brother, in fact.

Anyway, that's why I was at Grandma's, and one day she sent me up to the attic for some old clothes she had there in a binliner. She'd saved them for Oxfam or something and one of her friends was calling round to collect them. So up I trogged into this long dim attic, right? It was jam-packed with rubbish and I was in no rush, so I thought I'd poke about a bit, and that's how I found the bottle I'm going to tell you about. The bottle with the stuff in it. You don't have to listen if you don't want to.

There was no electric light up there. All there was was one dirty skylight in the slope of the roof. I found the binliner straight away. It was by the door. I left it there and started poking about. There was broken furniture, ancient household gadgets and tea-chests full of crockery, dusty glassware and mouldering clothes. There were small things on the floor to trip you up – piles of mildewed magazines, rusty flatirons and cracked vases. There was one roller skate. I'm not kidding – *one*. It must've belonged to Long John Silver or somebody. And a jam jar crammed with paint-brushes, and some stair rods and a pram and a handbag and a wire birdcage with a plastic budgie in it. I nearly crouched down and said *who's a pretty boy then?*, but I was frightened of getting my frock dirty.

Anyway, right at the back was a sort of cabinet with shelves on top and rows of tidgy drawers underneath. It looked really old. There was nothing on the shelves so I started opening drawers like somebody on the Antiques flipping Roadshow. There were sixteen of them – four rows of four. The top four were empty. They'll *all* be empty, I told myself, but I was wrong.

Third drawer along, second row, I struck gold. Well . . . glass. It was a bottle, flat in shape except for its round neck which had a cork in it. I picked it up and turned it in my hand. Thick blue glass like an old medicine bottle but no label. I held it up to the light. There was some stuff in it. Thickish liquid that moved like treacle. There wasn't much – about two centimetres. The cork had been pushed so far in I couldn't get a grip so I took it under the skylight and worked at it with my nails, and after a bit I got it out.

It came away with a pop. I sniffed it but it just smelt old so I sniffed the bottleneck. It smelt sort of sharp. Fruity. Bit like lime juice. It made my nostrils tingle, and the tingle seemed to pass behind my eyes into my forehead and then spread across the inside of my skull till it reached the nape of my neck and trickled down my spine.

It's hard to describe how it made me feel, and you wouldn't believe me anyway. I felt . . . excited. I was bursting with energy, like Popeye after a spinach fix. Ready for anything.

There was this mirror. A flyspecked full-length mirror that swivelled in a frame. I looked at myself. I thought I'd look different but I didn't so I stuck my tongue out. 'Just look at you,' I sneered. 'You're so *good*, aren't you, Jacqueline Hyde? So yuckily, sick-makingly good. See how *clean* you've kept yourself, even in this mucky old attic. Grandma *will* be pleased.'

I hated my reflection. *Hated* it. I know it sounds daft but I did. There was a flatiron on the floor. A rusty flatiron. I bent down and grabbed it and snarled, 'Here, Jacqueline Good – catch.' I got that mirror dead-centre and it shattered, spraying glittering fragments everywhere. The iron rebounded and crashed on the dusty floorboards

14

and I heard Grandma call out, 'Jacqueline –
what's happening up there? Are you all right?'

Oh, I was all right, all right. *More* than all right.
For the first time in my life I was *alive*. Fully alive.
I headed for the door.

Grandma was at the foot of the stairs. 'You've been ever such a long time dear,' she said as I started down. 'And what was that awful noise?'

'What noise?' I said. 'I didn't hear anything.'

'It was a loud thump,' she said, 'like something heavy falling over. You *must* have heard it.'

'No.' I brushed past her with a straight face but laughing inside and she said, 'You've forgotten the bag.'

I shook my head. 'I didn't forget, Gran.' She hates being called Gran. 'You can get it yourself – the exercise'll be good for your rheumatism.'

Outside, the rain had stopped. I turned left and set off walking. It must've been magic, the stuff

16

in that bottle. My mind was fantastically sharp. Colours seemed unnaturally bright. I was seeing things I wouldn't normally notice, like the way the sun glistened on the flagstones, walls and railings, and how puddles reflected bits of duck-egg blue. There were smells too – wet leaves and a whiff of some faraway bonfire, and I could feel sensations such as the breeze on my cheek and the rub of my shirt against my skin. When I breathed in, the cold air filled my lungs like silver light. I felt cool, strong and fearless as I motored on down, looking for fun.

I headed for the market. There's this market by the canal at Camden Lock. Loads of fancy stuff on little stalls. Candles. Jewellery. Ethnic clothes. It gets packed. There's drinks and hot grub too. I'd been there lots of times but not as Jacqueline Bad. That's what I was calling myself, by the way. Jacqueline Bad.

A mist hung over the black water as I boogied along the towpath. There weren't many people about and when I got to the market I found out why. It was shut. As soon as I saw the stripped-down stalls I remembered Grandma telling me once it was shut during the week. It's a weekend market.

I didn't care – not in the mood I was in. I just knew I'd find something interesting to do, and I did.

There's a big, two-storey building that was a warehouse when the canal was in use. It's all little shops now and they're closed when the market's shut. Some of the shops are on the upper floor. You get to them by going up some steps to a balcony. If you walk along this balcony past all the shops you come to some lavatories. I thought *they'd* be shut too, but they were open. Good-o, I said to myself.

There's this trick we sometimes play at school. Not *Jacqueline*, of course – she's far too good – but disruptives such as Craig Lampton. The trick is to cram great wodges of wet toilet paper in the plug-holes of all the washbasins and leave the taps running. If you do this when the caretaker isn't around and all the teachers are busy, the basins overflow and you get a flood which might reach the cloakroom or even the hall before anybody notices. It's brilliant.

I went in the women's. It was easy because the place was so quiet. With a full roll in one hand I worked my way along the row of gleaming basins, pulling paper, balling it in my fist, soaking it under the tap and packing it right down in the plughole. There were six basins, and I did the lot in about three minutes. It was a bit dodgy towards the end, when the hiss and splash of running water might mask the sound of someone approaching. I opened the door a crack and squinted out. All clear. I slipped out, cool and slow, closing the door behind me as the first basin brimmed over.

I looked over the balcony rail. Sparrows and pigeons picked placidly below. A cyclist sped by on the towpath. The High Street traffic roared softly in the background.

I could do the men's.

This felt dodgier because it was the men's, and because the effect of my sniff was wearing off, though I didn't realize that at the time. There were six basins again and I did a thorough job on the first two, but then I lost my cool and rushed the rest, skimping on paper so that the water seeped through and the basins took longer to fill. Doing the last one I could've sworn I heard footsteps. I shot into a cubicle and stood shaking behind the door but nobody came. While I was in there two basins overflowed and I had to wade to reach the door.

I walked away from the lavatories. There was still nobody about so I leaned on the balcony rail and closed my eyes. I could feel Jacqueline Bad seeping away. One minute it was cool to relax here while the lavatories flooded, and the next I wanted to be gone. I hurried down the stairs, crossed the market and walked up the ramp on to the High Street.

I'd just made the High Street when Jacqueline Good came back, and I was scared stiff. You'd think I'd murdered somebody, not just flooded some stupid lavatories. My knees went weak and I was shaking so much I had to stop and lean on the parapet to keep from falling over. I don't know *what* I thought was going to happen. I mean, even if somebody had found the flood already, there was nothing to connect it to me. I could've gone back to the towpath and strolled home the way I'd come and nothing would have happened, but I daren't. I went the long way round – along the High Street, right on to Delancey Street and up the slope to Parkway and

Gloucester Avenue. I even felt scared passing the steps I'd used getting down to the canal an hour ago.

With the steps behind me it was obvious I wasn't about to be arrested but I still felt bad. What was brilliant about swamping a washroom? Smashing an antique mirror? What was funny about telling an old lady the exercise'd be good for her rheumatism? I could hardly believe I'd done these things. They didn't seem funny in any way now that the sniff had worn off. I knew I'd have to face Grandma sooner or later and the prospect filled me with dread. If I'd had the bottle with me I'd have taken another sniff, but I'd put it down to pick up the flatiron. It was on the floor with all the bits of glass.

I won't bang on. I hung about till I got my courage up, and when I went indoors it wasn't nearly as bad as I'd expected. She wasn't blazing mad like I thought she'd be. She sat me down and brought tea and biscuits and asked me some questions. Was I fretting about something. Was I being bullied at school. Had I had a row with Mum and Dad. She seemed more worried than angry. I started apologizing about the mirror and what I'd said to her, and halfway through I burst into tears and she hugged me, which made me cry even more.

Anyway, that's how it started. Grandma had swept up the broken glass while I was out and the bottle had gone into the dustbin with it. If I'd left it there, or if the stuff had leaked out, the rest would never have happened and I wouldn't be stuck in this place but it's no good iffing, is it?

See – I *wanted* that bottle, even after the hassle I've just described. I couldn't forget the feeling that one little sniff had given me. It had only lasted an hour, but *what* an hour!

Don't get me wrong – I'd never fancied being bad. There were some really bad kids at school – disruptives – and it always seemed to me that the fun they got out of their antics wasn't worth the bother that nearly always followed. I mean – a flood now and then or a little fire – it's OK. It breaks the dull routine, but Craig Lampton and them – they were *forever* in detention or suspended or something. I thought it was stupid.

The bottle-buzz was something else though. I'd

christened it that, by the way – the bottle-buzz. It had blown my mind and I *had* to give it another go. The bottle had gone from the attic – I looked. There was just the cork, so I knew Grandma must've chucked it in the bin with the bits of mirror. What I did was, I sneaked out in the middle of the night. I *hate* the dark – always have – so *that* shows how hooked I was already. I crept down the yard at about two a.m. with the torch Grandma keeps on top of the fuse-box, and I found it. In the bin. I thought the treacly stuff would've spilled out for sure. I was ready to settle for a coating left on the inside – enough for a few more sniffs if I corked it tight – but I was lucky. Or unlucky, depending how you look at it. Anyway, the bottle had slipped down among some balls of screwed-up paper and was nearly upright. I fished it out and shone the torch on it and it looked like nothing had been lost at all, so I shoved the cork in and dropped it in my bathrobe pocket and crept back into the house.

I hid it in a shoe in the bottom of my wardrobe and got into bed. I slept OK, but I had this dream. I'll tell you about it if you like, only don't expect it to make sense. Dreams never do, do they?

It's night. In the dream, I mean. I'm walking along this street and I'm in a hurry. I'm scared but don't ask me why because I don't know. There are hardly any streetlights but it isn't that. It's like I need to *get* somewhere. Under cover, away from prying eyes. Yes – that's it. I remember now. Away from prying eyes.

Anyway, there I am, hurrying along and there's this alleyway leading off, and just as I'm crossing the mouth of the alley some kid – a little girl – comes hurtling out and runs smack into me. Well – I go berserk, don't I? I *know* the kid hasn't done it on purpose but I go flipping mad. I knock her over and start trampling her. I'm wearing these shiny boots with pointy toes and I stamp on her again and again and the thing is, I'm *enjoying* it.

She's not. She's screaming blue murder and people are coming so I run, and this one guy comes after me. I'm *really* motoring because I'm scared but I can't shake him off. In fact he's gaining on me. I hear his breath, and then this hand grabs my shoulder and I wake up screaming and that's it. I told you it didn't make sense.

What're you looking at me like *that* for?

Where were we? Oh yes – the dream. Well, I'd woken Grandma screaming like that and next morning, Tuesday, she said, are you absolutely *sure* you're not worrying about something, darling? This was at breakfast. I shook my head and she said, because you had a nightmare last night, do you remember? I said yes, I remembered, and she told me that nightmares are a sign that something's wrong. Changes in behaviour are another sign, she said, and I knew she meant the mirror and that. I didn't feel like telling her about the bottle. Well, she wouldn't have believed me, would she? *I* wouldn't, if I was her. So I said yes, there was something bothering me

29

and she said, what? Mum and Dad, I said. They don't care about me. All they care about is the shop.

Well, of course she said *nonsense*, like I knew she would. I said, if it's nonsense how come they load me onto you every holiday? Oh well, she said, they're very busy people. 'Tisn't easy you know, running a business these days.

There was more like that, then she said, you need taking out of yourself, my girl, and I was thinking, yes, well, maybe a good sniff'd fix that, but she said, I know. We'll have a day at the zoo. Take a picnic. We'll have a lovely time.

That's the trouble with grown-up relatives. They don't notice *you're* growing up, too. I mean, the zoo's OK when you're seven, but you don't want to be traipsing round with your grandma at eleven, sitting on the grass eating sandwiches.

Anyway, I couldn't get out of it so we went, and we didn't have a lovely time at all. *I* didn't. The weather was cool, with a wind fresh enough to make sitting out uncomfortable. Well, it *was* October. There were plenty of people about though, I'm not saying that. Some even ate picnics, huddled in anoraks with their backs to the wind. The kids who'd come with adults were all younger than me – eight or nine at the most. Kids my age were by themselves. I saw one bunch sniggering in my direction but they could've been laughing at something else.

There was a three-legged leopard. It had learned to get about without its missing forelimb but its movements were slow and graceless. It was no longer a typical example of its kind so why show it? It made me sad, which sums up the sort of day it was.

By three o'clock I was wishing I'd brought the bottle. I'd thought about it, but I was scared it might make me free the gorillas or feed Grandma to a Bengal tiger. I don't think it would have done, though. It'd have given me the guts to say, Grandma, I'm bored out of my skull. *You* can hang about gawping at emus if you want to – *I'm* off to find some real action.

Why didn't I say it anyway? Just come right out with it? 'Cause I was too *good*, that's why. I was Jacqueline Good, who let her gran drag her round all day in the freezing wind looking at a bunch of dumb animals she'd seen a thousand times on TV.

Gives a whole new meaning to the expression *no bottle*.

31

That was Tuesday. Wednesday, we went to Madame Tussauds and the Planetarium. We had to queue for both and when we got in it was nothing special. If this was Grandma's way of taking me out of myself it was a floparoo. Mind you, it was probably a terrific treat for *her*. She's Mum's mum, and a widow, and her idea of a wild time is church both morning *and* evening on a Sunday. I never knew my grandad, but I bet he didn't die of excitement.

Thursday, it bucketed down all day and we stayed in. Grandma spent the day baking because Mum and Dad were coming on Sunday to take me home. I wandered about the house picking up ornaments and putting them down. Grandma's got hundreds of ornaments. I looked out of blurry windows and flipped through some fusty old books. Looking back, I don't know how I lasted the pace.

Friday was a bit better. A bit. It was mainly dry, with a stiff breeze and a skyful of those little white clouds which turn mauve and orange when the sun goes down – and that's the end of my Michael Fish impression.

We went shopping. Not for gorgeous clothes like Kim at school though. Kim's my best friend by the way. Kim Farlow. You should see some of the stuff she wears. She looks like a model and her room's a branch of Next.

Gran and I did Sainsbury's and Marks and Spencer and the Post Office. I was being Jacqueline Good of course – reaching stuff down off high shelves and carrying heavy bags. I didn't get any clothes, but I *did* get a sticky bun and a Coke in Lite Bite when we'd finished.

Saturday, I did some hoovering. Grandma wanted the place clean for Mum and Dad. I went up to the attic again and looked through the rest of those little drawers but they were empty.

And that was it. Half-term. I can't pretend I

10

Sunday. Mum and Dad arrived in time for lunch. Mum kissed Grandma and hugged me. Dad pecked Grandma's cheek and looked at me. 'Nice time, sweetheart?'

'Yes, thanks.' Well – what *else* can you say?

'She's tired,' said Grandma. 'Been having nightmares, haven't you, darling?'

'One,' I said. 'One nightmare.' What did you have to go and mention *that* for, I thought. I could've strangled the old bat.

'Oh dear,' went Mum. 'What was it about, sweetie?'

'I don't remember.' I didn't feel like talking about it and I *detest* being called sweetie.

35

Lunch dragged. Dad banged on about the shop as usual. When Grandma brought the coffee I excused myself, pretending I hadn't finished packing. As I left the room I heard Mum say, she's such a *good* girl – so tidy, so considerate. I thought, you wouldn't say that if you'd seen the attic the other day. I hoped Grandma wasn't going to blab about *that.*

I went in Grandma's room and looked out the window. The Volvo was parked directly below. Drifts of leaves clogged the gutter. Trees in the square were half naked. Beyond them the sky looked sullen. See you in eight weeks, I said.

When I heard Mum and Dad getting their coats I grabbed my bag. I'd wrapped the bottle in a T-shirt and shoved it right down in a corner. I went downstairs. After another round of hugs and kisses we were off, me twisting round in the back seat to wave to Grandma. She couldn't help being a crumbly and she hadn't mentioned the mirror.

Well, Jacqueline Bad, I thought, I wonder how you'll get on in Wexham. And what will you reckon to *school*? For once, I was looking forward to school.

11

'What did you do at your Grandma's, Jacqueline?' It was five to nine, but in that brand-new black leather jacket with all the zips and pockets, Kim was definitely out of uniform. I was dead jealous. I was dying to tell her about the bottle, but Grandma says anticipation is sometimes the best part of a treat so I controlled myself. 'I hung around. Watched telly. Oh – and we went to the zoo. How about you?'

I *swear* I didn't do it on purpose. Zoo and you, I mean, but Kim latched onto it and broke into a dance. '*We went to the zoo, zoo, zoo. How about you, you, you . . .*' The backpack she carried bounced up and down as she moved.

I felt myself go red. 'OK – I *know* you did cooler stuff than me. You always do, so stop pratting about and tell me.'

'Well . . .' She stopped dancing and pretended to think. 'I went to Next for one thing. Got this jacket. And my cousin Natasha – she's sixteen – took me ice-skating and afterwards we ate at this Italian place she knows. Dead sophisticated. And – let me see – I went to Pictureville with Mum to see Kevin Costner. That was after we had our hair done at *Oh, Them Golden Snippers*. And the next night it rained so we had pizzas delivered and watched videos till one.'

'One in the *morning*?'

Kim nodded. 'Uh-huh. And that's about all, I think.'

'*All*?' If I was jealous before, I was positively *green* now. 'You poor thing. It's a wonder you didn't die of boredom.'

The buzzer went. Kim pulled a regulation blazer out of her backpack and stuffed the leather jacket in. 'Oh well,' she sighed, straightening up and swinging the pack over her shoulder. 'If that was October break, roll on Christmas.'

Eleven o'clock. English with Mr Whittaker. Write me an essay, he said. The Best Day of my Break. Dead original, eh? Why is it that whenever something good happens at school – a trip, a visitor, a holiday – they go and spoil it by making you *write* about it?

The Best Day of my Break. Well – we *all* know which day *that* was, don't we? For me, I mean. That's right – Monday. The day I did the bogs. Question is, dared I *write* about it? Remember I was Jacqueline Good at the time, and Jacqueline Good never took a chance. On the other hand she didn't tell lies, and if she wrote about some *other* day – the zoo for instance – she'd be lying, right?

I decided to give it a shot. A few lines. If it looked too bad I could always scribble it out and write about the wild time I had with Grandma at Madame Tussauds.

The best day of my break was last Monday when I found an old bottle and discovered my other self. Jacqueline Bad's her name and she knows where the fun is. I wrote this and was reading it through, trying to decide if I dared hand it in, when old Nitwit cleared his throat behind me. Nitwit's what we call old Whittaker, and he has this habit of creeping about the room while we're busy. I nearly jumped out of my skin.

'If I had wanted fantasy, Jacqueline Hyde, I'd have asked for it.' Everybody giggled. I felt my cheeks burn. 'You are to give me a factual account – *factual*, mind – of your chosen day. Strike out that nonsense and start again, please.'

'But, sir . . .'

'No buts, Jacqueline. You disappoint me. It's not like you to disregard instructions. Start again.'

He moved on. I got my ruler out and drew a diagonal line through my work, thinking, what the heck am I *supposed* to write if I can't write the truth?

40

I was shoving the ruler back in my bag when it clicked against something hard. I looked all round. Nitwit was two tables away. Everyone else was writing. I fished about for the bottle, watching the teacher all the time. When he bent over Kylie Barraclough I pulled it out, uncorked it and took a quick sniff. By the time he straightened up, the bottle was back in the bag and weird things were happening inside my skull. I picked up my pen and wrote rapidly, filling line after line, till I'd done one and a half pages. I read it through. The handwriting was rubbish but the stuff itself was absolutely brilliant. I couldn't believe it was mine.

'Finished, have we, Jacqueline?' said Nitwit.

'Yessir.'

'That was quick. Bring it out then – let's have a look. And *do* take that silly grin off your face, girl. You look like something that's escaped from the loony bin.'

There's three lights above old Trubshaw's door.
The traffic lights, we call 'em. Trubshaw's the
Head, by the way. What you do is, you knock on
the door and watch the lights. Red means go
away, I'm busy. Amber means wait a minute,
and green means come in. I got a green but I
didn't care. I trogged in, clutching my so-called
essay.

'Yes, Jacqueline?' he beamed. Adults always
beam at me.

'Please, sir, Mr Whittaker sent me with my
essay.'

'Ah.' He held out his hand. 'Let me see.' He was

practically reaching for a commendation slip. I put the two sheets in his hand and watched him start to read.

Halfway down page one he went pale and stopped. He made a little noise in his throat and looked up. 'Is this your work, Jacqueline?'

'Yessir.'

'I . . . are you *ill*, child? Has something happened at home?'

'No, sir.'

'Then . . .' He flicked the papers with the nails of his free hand. 'Why *this*, Jacqueline?'

'It's the truth, sir, and you've got to admit it's good.'

That was a mistake. He went ape-shape. 'I admit no such thing, girl. There's nothing good about it. I cannot understand why you would write stuff like this and . . .' He broke off and read aloud:

The day was cold and rotten and we'd sugar-all to do,
So Grandma packed a rotten lunch and dragged me to
*   the zoo.*
We saw some crummy emus and some crummy emu
*   eggs,*

43

*And we saw a beat-up leopard and it only had three
    legs.*
*We ate a rotten picnic though the wind was wild and
    free*
*And some kids were rotten laughing and I know they
    laughed at me.*
*We saw some Bengal tigers and some bears in rotten
    pits*
*And I wished they'd pull my grandma down and rip
    her all to bits . . .*

He stopped and looked up at me and I knew
my sniff must be wearing off 'cause I was feeling nervous. 'This is totally unacceptable,
Jacqueline,' he murmured. The Trub's at his
most dangerous when he talks quietly. 'And I
won't have it. I ought to show this to your parents, but in view of your previous excellent
record I'm going to give you a chance to make
amends.' He gazed at me. 'I can see from your
face that you are anxious to make amends, so
this is what you will do. You will apologize to
Mr Whittaker and spend your lunchtime pro-
ducing an outstanding essay on the same subject
in your neatest hand, and I shall expect to see

you here at one-thirty precisely with the finished piece. Is that clear?'

'Yessir.'

Jacqueline Good was back, and she fled.

'Hey, Jackie!' It was hometime and I was crossing the yard. I turned and saw Craig Lampton hurrying to catch me up. I was amazed. Jackie, he'd called me. As the school's number one disruptive, Craig hated me. Teacher's pet was his usual name for me. That or frogface.

He grinned, drawing level. 'What did you put, Jackie?'

'It's Jacqueline,' I told him, 'and I don't know what you mean.'

'In your *essay*, you div. What did you put?'

'Nothing.'

'It *can't* have been nothing – you had to see Trub and do it again. Come on – tell us.'

'No.' I didn't feel like discussing it with Craig. I was through the gateway by this time but he fell in beside me. I looked at him. 'You live the other way, don't you?'

'Tell us,' he wheedled. 'Then I'll go.'

'Oh, all right.' I couldn't be bothered arguing so I recited the bit I knew by heart – the bit old Trub read out. When I'd finished, Craig said, 'You never wrote that.'

'I did.'

'You didn't.'

'What's the point of asking if you're not going to believe me, thickhead?' I didn't blame him though. I could hardly believe it myself.

'D'you wanna be in my gang?'

'What?'

'My gang. You can join if you want.'

'I dunno.' All the nuts were in his gang. Glenys Baxter. Mary-Beth Summerscales. Anthony Netherwood and Colin Wexley. I was sort of pleased to be asked though. The Lampton Gang ruled at Church Lane Middle School. Loads of kids wanted to be in it. 'I'll think about it.'

Craig grinned. 'OK. See you tomorrow then, Jacqueline.'

'See you, Craig.'

It wasn't *me* he wanted in his gang of course – it was Jacqueline Bad, but that was all right. As long as I had my bottle I could fetch her whenever I wanted, couldn't I?

15

'Good day at school, darling?' Mum was peeling potatoes at the sink.

I snorted. 'Did *you* ever have a good day at school, Mum?'

'Well . . .' Mum smiled. 'It seems so, looking back, but then we tend to forget the bad bits, don't we?'

'I won't.' I was thinking about the apology I'd had to make to Nitwit and how I'd had to rewrite that stupid essay, but of course I wasn't going to tell Mum about that. I got a Coke from the fridge and leaned on the drainer, swigging out of the can.

'I *wish* you'd use a glass, darling.'

'Why, Mum? Can's OK. Saves washing up, doesn't it?'

'Well, yes, but . . .'

'Well, there you are then.'

Mum looked at me. 'Are you *all right*, dear?'

'How d'you mean?'

'You're not – ill or anything, are you?'

'You're the *second* person who's asked me that today, Mum. I'm fine.'

'Hmmm. It's just that you've always *loved* school, Jacqueline. Couldn't wait to get there. You seem . . . less keen somehow.'

'Yeah, well. I'm so good, all the teachers love me and all the kids hate me. Did you know the kids hated me, Mum?'

'No, dear, I did not, and I think you're mistaken. Some might envy you all the commendations you get, but I don't believe they hate you. Kim Farlow's a good friend isn't she?'

I shrugged. 'Kim needs someone to show off to with her clothes and stuff. I make the right admiring noises.'

Mum looked at me. 'What a cynical thing to say, Jacqueline. Are you . . . worried about anything, dear?'

'Not a thing. Why?'

'Well . . . Grandma says your behaviour last week was a bit odd. She mentioned bullying. *Are* you being bullied, darling?'

''Course not.' I smiled. 'And I certainly won't be now.'

Mum dumped the potatoes into a pan of water and lit the gas. 'Whatever do you mean?'

'I mean I've got protection, Mum, if I want it.'

'Protection? I don't care for the sound of that, darling. Reminds me of Chicago in the gangster era. I hope you're not getting into bad company.'

I drained the can and dropped it in the bin. 'Who, me? What sort of bad company would want a good little girl like me around, Mum?' I didn't wait for an answer. I went up to my room to play music and think about Craig Lampton's invitation.

16

That night I had another dream. Again I was hurrying through silent streets, this time in brilliant moonlight. I was nearly where I wanted to be when I saw this old guy coming towards me. He was wearing a top hat and walking with a stick. I hadn't wanted anyone to see me, so the sight of him made me blazing mad. Why did *he* have to be in this particular spot at this very minute? What was he *doing*, doddering about in the middle of the night anyway? I ducked my head and put on a spurt, hoping to get past without either of us saying anything but it was no good. I was just about to pass him when he said excuse me and stuck himself smack in front of me so I couldn't get by. I eyeballed him. 'Yes – what is it?'

'Such a beautiful night,' he went. 'Did you ever see such a moon?'

'What do you *want*? I'm in a hurry.'

He bowed. I'm not kidding. I'd just practically bitten his head off and he bowed like I was a princess. Or a prince, because I think I was a guy in the dream. 'I apologize, sir, for encroaching on your time. The fact is, I set out for a stroll after dinner and lost my way.' He chuckled. 'Bewitched by the moon, perhaps. I wonder if you would be so good as to direct me to Villiers Street?'

'I've never *heard* of it.' I tried to get past him but he blocked me again.

'It's off the Strand, sir. Perhaps you could direct me to the *Strand*?'

I was getting madder by the second. 'Step aside this instant, sir, or I'll direct you straight to Hell.'

That's what I said. I remember it clearly. I don't know where I was getting the fancy talk from, but stuff like that happens in dreams, doesn't it?

He was surprised, I can tell you. He backed off

quick and said, 'My good man' – so I *was* a guy in the dream – 'My good man, I'm sure there is no call for that sort of . . .'

'Damn you, get out of my way!' I lost it completely – started hitting him with my stick. I had this walking stick, quite heavy, and I laid into him with it, knocking his top hat off. He had long silver hair which shone in the moonlight. I remember that. And he fell down and I just kept clubbing him till he stopped moving and my stick broke in two. I stood looking down at him and then I felt eyes on me and looked up, and a girl was staring at me from an upstairs window. A girl in white.

I screamed. Not just in the dream but in real life too. Mum came and put the light on and sat on the bed, hugging me. Rocking me. 'I killed him, Mum,' I said, 'and she *saw* me. The girl in white.'

Mum hugged me tight. 'You *dreamed* it, sweetheart. It isn't real. It's gone now – all gone. I'm here. Daddy's here. We love you, darling. Lie down now. Lie down. *That's* my girl. That's my good, good girl.'

But it wasn't, Mum. It wasn't.

I was dead knackered next morning. I trogged through the school gate like a zombie and there was Craig Lampton with two of his sidekicks – Glenys Baxter and Anthony Netherwood. These three had more suspensions between them than a shark has teeth. 'Here she is,' said Craig. He had a stupid grin on his face. 'Tell 'em what you put, Jacqueline.'

I looked at him. 'You know what I put. *You* tell 'em.'

'I can't remember it all.'

So I recited what I could remember. Glenys and Anthony listened, and when I was through, they capered about, laughing at the tops of their voices. 'Nice one, Jackie,' whooped Glenys. She knew very well I don't get called Jackie, and she seemed to have forgotten how she had filled my bag with horse manure on the way home a couple of weeks ago for getting a commendation.

Anthony leered. 'Is it right you're joining the gang, then?'

'I dunno. Maybe. I'm thinking about it.'

'"*Course* she's joining,' said Craig. 'She'll have to do a dare, though.'

'I thought the *essay* counted as my dare.'

'No way. *I* set the dares.'

I pulled a face. Maybe I could stand not being in his gang after all. 'What sort of dare, then?'

He made a big show of thinking hard. '*I* know,' he said, 'you can do the roof-goof.'

'What the heck's that?' I didn't like the sound of it.

'It's nothing major. You get on the roof and knock on that plastic bubble over Trubshaw's office, and when he looks up you stick your tongue out. Anthony got suspended for it last term.'

'*I* don't want to get suspended. My dad'll kill me.'

'He won't suspend *you*. You've got about six million commendations. What d'you say?'

The other two were watching me. I still wasn't sure I even wanted to be in the gang, but it was a sort of honour to be *asked* if you know what I mean – especially to a wimp like Jacqueline Good, so I nodded. 'OK. When?' Glenys and Anthony cheered which made me feel great, but I was going to need a really good sniff before I did it.

'Hometime this aft. He'll be in there then, settling down with his pipe for a bit of peace.' Mr Trubshaw never smoked while there were children in school.

I nodded. 'OK, you're on. I only hope you're right about my not getting suspended.'

He winked. 'Trust me.' What a veg. I'd sooner trust a rottweiler but it was too late – I was committed.

18

It was a *brilliant* feeling being Jacqueline Bad, because your *memory* didn't go. You could be reckless and fearless and you didn't give a monkey's about anything, but at the same time you *knew* you weren't *really* like that. Jacqueline *Good* was there, you see, just underneath, watching. And she would be *horrified*. She wanted to stop you. You could *feel* her trying to pull you back, only the sniff had weakened her. And *that* was the difference, because Jacqueline Bad was there *all* the time you see – even when I *didn't* sniff. She was there before I knew there *was* a bottle, but she was weak. She'd sometimes try to get me to do things – bad things – but

Jacqueline Good was always too strong for her. The stuff in that bottle *reversed* the situation, so that Jacqueline *Bad* was the strong one. I *know* you haven't a clue what I'm banging on about so you'll just have to take my word, but it was a brilliant feeling.

Anyway, at hometime on this day I'm telling you about, we were loitering in the space between the main building and the shed where sports and gardening equipment are kept. It was twenty past four. All the other kids had gone and so had some of the teachers. The Lampton Gang was all present though, which meant that Craig, Glenys and Anthony had been joined by Colin Wexley and Mary-Beth Summerscales. I'd taken a big sniff at four o'clock in the toilets. I was dying to get started. 'What do I do after?' I asked.

Craig grinned. 'When he's seen you, you run to the corner nearest the gate and jump off. It's not high. You'll be halfway home before old Trub reaches the door.'

'No cheating,' put in Glenys. 'Remember he has to *see* you with your tongue out.' She's a complete prat, Glenys.

I eyeballed her. 'I *know*, motormouth. Give us a leg up.'

The building was one of those low ones with a flat roof, but it seemed a long way down when you were up there. I looked across the expanse of patched green felt. Five dome-shaped plastic bubbles admitted daylight to various parts of the school. I worked out which one was over the Head's office and headed towards it on tiptoe. It was important to get the job done because I might easily be spotted by a departing teacher. The roof gave slightly under my tread. I pictured myself plunging through onto Trub's desk and saying, you wanted to see me, sir?

The bubble had a film of muck. I knelt down and used my sleeve to rub myself a face-size window. The desk was directly under the bubble and I had a perfect view of Trubshaw's bald patch as he relaxed in his padded swivel chair, filling his pipe. He hadn't heard me rubbing off the dirt and he didn't notice the faint shadow I cast on his blotter. I wasn't a bit scared, though Jacqueline Good was doing her best to pull me away. I made a fist of my right hand and rapped on the bubble.

The effect was stupendous. He'd just struck a match, and his violent start caused him to drop it into his lap along with the pipe and a small avalanche of tobacco. He leapt to his feet and beat at the front of his trousers with both hands while looking wildly about him for the source of the noise. I gave him a second or two, then rapped again. This time he looked up and we locked eyes and I stuck my tongue so far out it touched the bubble. I held my pose just long enough to see his mouth fall open, then I was up and away, pounding across the felt. I didn't even *think* about the drop. I launched myself out and down, hitting the tarmac so hard it stung, pelting down the driveway where the others were already in full flight.

19

He phoned Mum. The Trub I mean. She was getting the tea ready and he phoned her. She was talking to him when I got in but I didn't know. The phone's in the front room. There was just this half-chopped lettuce and a panful of spuds and no Mum so I got myself a Coke and sat down. The sniff hadn't worn off yet so I was dead cool.

When she came in I said, 'What's up?' I could tell by her face *something* was.

She gazed at me. 'I've just had Mr Trubshaw on the phone, Jacqueline. Where have you been?'

'School, of course.'

'*After* school, I mean. You're a bit late.'

I shrugged; so cool it wasn't true. Jacqueline Good would've been wetting her pants. 'Coming along. Talking. You know.'

'Who with?'

'Glenys. Mary-Beth. What *is* this, anyway?'

'Mr Trubshaw believes he might have seen you on the school roof a short time ago. Is he right, Jacqueline?'

'Are you kidding, Mum?' I was magnificent, though I say it myself. '*Me* on the roof – can you imagine it?'

'Well, frankly, no, but . . .'

'There you are, then. *You* can't imagine it, Trub *can*. He's got an overdeveloped imagination.'

'Mr Trubshaw is a very competent headmaster and a gentleman, too,' said Mum. '*Somebody* pulled a face at him through his skylight, and if I find out it was you, you'll find yourself in very serious trouble, young woman.'

'You won't.'

'I won't what?'

'Find out it was me.'

'I certainly hope not, Jacqueline. I'll have to mention Mr Trubshaw's call to Daddy, though.'

'Good. It'll give you both something to talk about besides the shop.'

'That's a *very* impudent remark, Jacqueline. You've changed, and not for the better. Your father puts it down to hormones and I hope he's right. *I* suspect you're getting into bad company.'

'No.' I shook my head. 'If Dad says it's hormones, it's hormones. He's infallible, my dad. Not like old Trub. *He*'ll be seeing pixies next, I shouldn't wonder.'

20

Dad wasn't all that interested, as it turned out. The shop was going through a bad patch and he had more important things to think about. All he said was, see to it, Sandra, can't you – I'm up to my neck as it is.

I was dead relieved. The sniff had practically worn off by the time he got home, and Jacqueline Good would've caved in and confessed if he'd applied the third degree.

After the meal I went to my room and locked the door. I wasn't feeling too good if you must know. It had something to do with the bottle. I'd noticed before that when the effect wore off, I didn't just go back to normal. For hours afterwards I'd feel *worse* than normal. Bored. Depressed. Ready to burst into tears at the slightest thing. At these times I just wanted to take another sniff. I knew *that*'d make me feel alright, but I daren't do it. I was frightened I'd get hooked. Not be able to stop. The buzz was brilliant but I had to stay in control.

I put a CD on and lay on the bed with my hands behind my head, staring at the ceiling. I talked to myself. Told myself everything was fine. Wasn't I the new hero of the Lampton Gang? Sure I was. I'd bluff it out with old Trubshaw tomorrow and be the envy of the school, even if Kim showed up in a whole new outfit.

See . . . I could kid myself while I was awake, but there was no escaping the dream. I had it again that night, and it was the worst yet. It started where the last one left off. I can *see* you don't believe me, but it did. The white-haired guy was on the ground and the girl in white was staring down at me and I ran. I ran till I came to a dark room and locked myself in, but I could hear people moving about outside. I don't know who they were but I was scared of them and they *knew* I was in there. I kept dead quiet, hoping they'd go away, but something hit the door with a terrific bang and I woke up, and I could hear the echo of that bang even though I was awake. I don't think I screamed, because nobody came, but I was shivering like mad and I daren't let myself go back to sleep. They were waiting for me, see?

What d'you keep *writing* on that pad?

21

Wednesday morning, Craig and Mary-Beth were waiting by the gate. I looked at them. 'Am I in, then?'

Craig grinned. 'Sure are. You did brilliant.'

'*Loved* the way you jumped,' said Mary-Beth. 'Like a flipping racehorse.'

'Trub called my mum.'

'He *didn't*?'

'He did. Wasn't sure it was me though, and Mum told him it probably wasn't.'

Mary-Beth pulled a face. 'You're lucky. When he called *my* mum after I painted the guinea pig, she said, oh yes, that'll be Mary-Beth. She's got a warped sense of humour.'

Craig looked at me. 'He'll have you in though, and you'll need to watch it. He's got a quiet way of talking to you that makes you *want* to own up. You think, how can I lie to such a gentle, reasonable guy? I nearly admitted setting fire to the caretaker once.'

Sure enough, at the end of assembly, Trub said, I want to see Jacqueline Hyde in my office immediately after registration. I knocked at twenty to ten and got the green light. 'You wanted to see me sir?' I tried to sound dead mystified.

'Yes, Jacqueline. Stick out your tongue, please.'

'Sir?'

'Your tongue, girl. Stick it out.'

I did, but not as far as yesterday. He looked at it. 'Hmmm. Is this the first time you've shown me your tongue this week, Jacqueline?'

'Y . . . yessir. First time *ever*, I think, sir.'

'I didn't see it up *there* then, after school yesterday?' He jabbed a finger at the skylight.

'Sir?' I looked at him like I thought he'd lost his marbles.

'I assume your mother told you I called her, Jacqueline?'

'Yessir.'

'And you're saying it *wasn't* you I saw on the roof at four twenty-five yesterday?'

'The *roof*, sir? Me? No, sir . . . I've *never* been on the roof.'

'Hmmm. Where *were* you at four twenty-five, Jacqueline?'

'Walking home sir, with Glenys Baxter and Mary-Beth Summerscales.'

'And I suppose they'd confirm that if I asked them?'

'I'm sure they would, sir.'

'Yes, Jacqueline, so am I.' He sighed. 'Very well, off you go.'

I had the door open when he said, 'Oh, and Jacqueline?'

I turned. 'Sir?'

'We can't choose our family but we choose our friends, and it's an important choice. Think about it.'

'Yessir.'

22

At breaktime, Kim said, 'What did old Trubshaw want, Jacqueline?' She'd taken off her school shoes and was wearing a pair of shiny black boots with brilliant pink laces.

'Oh, nothing. He thought he saw me on the roof but it was somebody else.'

She looked at me. '*I* heard it was you from Kirsty Mapplebeck.'

'Was it, heck.'

'No, well I *told* her. I said, Jacqueline doesn't do stuff like that, but it's got around that you did. In fact you're quite a hero today in some circles.'

'Yeah, well.' It felt good, but I didn't want to

attract *too* much attention. 'Where'd you get the boots?'

'Tramplers in town. Like 'em?'

'Mmm – *mmm*. Is it your birthday or something?' I knew it wasn't.

'No. My mum just saw them and I liked them so she bought them. What're you doing Saturday?'

I shrugged. 'Dunno. Probably end up shopping with my mum.'

'Oh, yawn, yawn. I thought I'd go to the Pavilion for a Coke, see who turns up.' The Pavilion's a wooden cafe in the local park where kids gather most weekends.

I pulled a face. 'Sounds good. Wish I was doing the same.'

'Ask your mum. She doesn't need you along, does she? I mean, you're not getting clothes or anything?' She *knew* I wasn't, the little cow.

'Ha – that'll be the day.'

'Ask her, then. Give me a ring tonight.'

'OK.'

At lunchtime, Craig said, 'What you doing Saturday, Jackie?'

'Depends. I might go to the Pavilion with Kim. And the name's *Jacqueline*.'

'Ooo – wow! Sure you can stand the excitement, *Jacqueline*?'

'Why – what're *you* doing?'

He grinned. 'We'll be in the park too, but not in the cafe.'

'Where, then?'

'Greenhouse. We've a job to do there.'

'A job? What sort of job?' The greenhouse was a huge glass and iron structure from Victorian times in which grew orchids, palms, tree-ferns and other exotic plants. You could go in and walk a narrow winding path and it was like being in the jungle – hot and moist and smelly with great, fleshy, vivid leaves that brushed your face and hands and left them wet. It was easy to imagine snakes and tigers and poisonous spiders lurking in that dim green wilderness, but of course there were none. The only dangerous beast in the greenhouse was Selwyn Tordoff the gardener, who loved plants more than people and watched visitors like a hawk – especially kids.

Craig chuckled. 'Old Selwyn kicked us out last week. Threatened us with the cops. We're gonna get even.'

'How?'

73

'Come along and find out. You're one of us, aren't you?'

'Sure.'

'Well, then. Half-nine by the paddling pool. And don't be late.'

'Mum?'

'Yes, dear?'

'What're you doing tomorrow?' It was Friday teatime. Dad wasn't home yet.

'Oh – Daddy needs me at the shop in the morning. Mountains of paperwork. You can come too if you like.'

'Oh, Mu-um. Do I *have* to?' The shop, otherwise known as Office Electronics is a really boring place to spend time. You've got to be quiet and stay out of the way, which means sitting in the storeroom at the back. There isn't even a TV.

'No, of course you don't *have* to, Jacqueline. What will you do instead?'

'Dunno. Watch telly I suppose. Or I might call for Kim and go to the park.'

'Well, be careful. Don't . . .'

'Talk to any strange men,' I finished for her. She says that every time I mention the park.

Later, in my room I lay on the floor thinking about what Trub had said. We choose our friends. He meant the Lampton Gang, of course. He was sharp for a crumbly and must've spotted me with Craig. He'd rather I stuck with Kim and Kirsty and kids like that – the quiet, clever set who did as they were told and were no trouble. Well – that was fine for Jacqueline Good. Always had been, but it wouldn't do for Jacqueline Bad at all, and that was where Trubshaw *wasn't* so sharp. He didn't even know Jacqueline Bad existed.

So the question was, who should I be tomorrow? I always had a decent time with Kim, even if she *was* a show-off. Especially at the Pavilion, but . . . well, I'd done it all before, right? Whereas Craig's stunt was bound to be something completely new: the sort of thing Jacqueline Good wouldn't dream of getting mixed up in. But Jacqueline *Bad* . . . Jacqueline Bad would probably turn out to be the most daring guy in the gang, and that would *really* be something, wouldn't it?

The CD faded out. I could hear Mum and Dad arguing downstairs. They were forever arguing those days. I blamed the shop. I got up, put on another CD to drown them out and lay on the bed, wishing a tall, good-looking pop star would climb through my window that minute and carry me away to his gorgeous oceanside mansion in California, but that stuff never happens in real life, does it? Still, I was luckier than most. At least I could leave my boring life now and then, and have a go at being somebody else. I was going to do it, too. Tomorrow.

24

They were all waiting when I got to the paddling pool. It was twenty-five to ten. I hadn't phoned Kim Wednesday night and we hadn't spoken since, so she'd assume I was in Wexham with Mum. I'd taken a good old sniff among the rhododendrons so I was set to boogie.

Craig frowned, the dummy. 'You're late.'

'I know. I came the long way round.'

'What for?' demanded Anthony.

I gave him the stare. The Jacqueline Bad special. 'So I wouldn't bump into Kim. Not that it's any of your business, Netherwood.'

The others laughed and Mary-Beth said,

'That's right, *Netherwood* – keep your sticky beak out of other people's business, why don't you?'

'OK, OK,' interrupted Craig. 'That's enough. Old Selwyn'll have opened up and gone now. Let's do it.'

It was a typical November morning: mist and wet grass and beads on the spider webs. We saw a jogger on a distant path and an old guy walking a terrier, but there was nobody anywhere near the greenhouse. You were supposed to close the door as soon as you were inside to preserve the heat but Craig said, 'Colin, stand in the doorway and yell if you see anyone coming.' He turned to the rest of us and nodded towards the waist-high shelf which ran all the way round the structure between the windows and the pathway. The shelf was crammed four rows deep with terracotta pots, each row standing a little higher than the row in front. In the summertime these pots held full-grown flowering plants, so that the shelf was invisible under a cascade of riotous blooms which drenched the humid atmosphere with their perfume. The moment a bloom began to fade its pot was whipped away by Selwyn and replaced. Crumblies drove miles on summer weekends just to stroll through the greenhouse feasting their senses on Selwyn's symphony of hues and heady scents. I read that last bit in the local rag. Good, eh?

But this was November and the pots held seedlings. Selwyn's delicate babies. Hundreds of them, each one patiently pricked out by his own loving hands to be pampered through the coming winter with food and heat and moisture so that next summer's display might be every bit as spectacular as the last. And it was towards these seedlings that Craig Lampton nodded.

'I want 'em out. Pulled up, every one of 'em, chucked on the path and trampled. When old Selwyn comes back I want him to find nothing but empty pots. You got that?'

It was then I had my brilliant idea. 'Hang on,' I said. 'Wouldn't it be funnier if he came back and found them planted *upside down* with their roots in the air?'

There was a brief silence as the gang members took this in, then Glenys let out a whoop. '*Brill*!' she cried. 'Can't you just *see* the silly old plonker's face when he walks in and sees . . .'

'Yeah!' A slow grin spread over Craig's face as the others started chuckling. He nodded and punched me in the arm. 'Brilliant, kid. I don't know how you dream 'em up, I really don't. He'll think he's gone bananas – planted 'em that way himself. It's *awesome*, is what it is.'

So that's what we did. It took ages. Colin kept watch all the time but nobody came, so we were lucky. When every seedling was standing on its head we stood looking at them, killing ourselves laughing. Then we trooped out and faded into the mist, leaving the door wide open.

I can't tell you *exactly* what happened next because I wasn't there, but there was some stuff in the local rag and also gossip, and I can make a fair stab at why Selwyn didn't go back to the greenhouse that night even though frost was forecast.

He found this tramp, see? This vagrant. It was dusk, and Selwyn was clopping along the path on his way to lock up the greenhouse and the gate at the far end of the park, when he saw a flicker of light coming from that dilapidated summer-house which stands on rotting stilts among the rhododendrons. He switched on his torch and called hello, and a voice answered and there was this guy inside on the bench under some cardboard, shielding his eyes from the torchlight with his hand. Selwyn told him the park closed at dusk and the guy said he wasn't doing any harm. He was smoking a fag, and Selwyn said he might burn the place down. The guy laughed and said the timber was so sodden you couldn't set it alight with a flame-thrower. It was all in the paper when the guy came up for trial. Anyway, in the end Selwyn told him he could spend the night as long as he moved on at first light. The guy wasn't a bit grateful – said he'd fought for this country, and he tried to make Selwyn bring him grub and ciggies and something to drink. He even asked the poor dope for the *cap* he was wearing. He didn't get it. He got four months in the slammer instead. Criminal damage to the greenhouse, but that was later.

See – talking to this guy made old Selwyn *forget* about the greenhouse, first time in his life. He must've thought he'd locked it already or something because he went on and did the far gate, then went home. And that's how the frost got in and killed all of the tropical plants, some of which had been there since eighteen seventy-something. Crying shame, if you ask me. And

26

I didn't get away with it altogether though, because the minute I fell asleep that night I was back in the dream and those guys were waiting for me just like I told you they'd be. I was inside and they were outside but they were battering the door and I knew the lock wouldn't hold. I was petrified. Well – I was a murderer, see? I *knew* the old guy with the silver hair was dead, and the girl in white had watched me club him. She was a witness. If those guys got in I'd hang for sure. Yes, hang. I know we don't *have* hanging any more, but in the place *I* was going at night they hung guys all the time.

That cabinet was in the dream. The one in

Grandma's attic. As the guys assaulted the door I was rooting through the drawers in a panic, looking for something. I don't know what it was – only that it was terrifically important. And just as I found it . . . I think it was something in a bottle . . . and no, it wasn't *that* bottle . . . just as I laid my hand on it there was a splintering crash and I knew it was too late.

I woke myself yelling and I woke Mum, too. I couldn't stop shaking and she hugged me like before, saying what *is* it darling . . . what is it that frightens you so badly? You can tell Mummy . . .

So I did. I told her about hurrying through little streets, not wanting to be seen. Keeping to the shadows. I'm a guy, I said. I told how the kid comes hurtling out of the alley and how I knock her down and trample her, and how this guy chases me and I wake up just as I'm nearly caught. And I told about the white-haired man who asks me the way and I club him and the girl in white, gazing down. And finally I told her I'm in a locked room, hiding, and these men know I'm in there and they're battering the door down and I can't find . . . I can't find . . .

I didn't mention any bottle. I was upset, but not *that* upset. Oh – and I told her the guys're shouting something. The guys outside the door. Checkle, they yell. Checkle, checkle, checkle.

When I told this bit, Mum held me at arm's length, looked into my eyes and said, 'When you were at Grandma's, Jacqueline, were you by any chance *reading* something?' I just looked at her. 'A book,' she said. 'Did you try one of Grandma's books, and did it frighten you?'

I shook my head. 'No, Mum. I didn't read anything, and if I *had* it wouldn't have frightened me. Why d'you ask?'

'I'm ... I'm trying to find out what's caused you to start having nightmares, darling. You never *used* to.'

I knew the cause, but I'd no intention of telling Mum. I was hooked on the buzz, though I wasn't admitting it at the time, not even to myself, and I didn't want the bottle taken away. She tucked me in and kissed me and I felt quite rotten deceiving her, but I hadn't actually lied, and anyway, we *all* tell porkies sometimes, don't we?

'Course we do.

Kim phoned at ten the next morning. Dad picked up. He covered the mouthpiece with his hand and yelled for me.

I had a moment of panic. The greenhouse. Surely they hadn't found out . . .

'It's Kim.' He handed me the phone.

'Hi, Kim. How's it hanging?'

'OK. You doing anything?'

'Nothing special. Why?'

'Well, it's a nice day. I wondered if you'd fancy meeting me at the Pavilion for a Coke.'

'You were going there *yesterday*, for Pete's sake. What've you done – fallen in love with old

Doris?' Doris runs the Pavilion. She must be about seventy.

'Oh, sure – she's my fairy godmother. No, it'll be something to do, that's all. What d'you say?'

'OK. What time?'

'Eleven?'

'See you then.'

'See you.'

I had this interesting idea as I was fixing my hair. Two ideas. I smiled at myself in the mirror. We could walk by the greenhouse, see if old Selwyn was about. *And* I'd take the bottle along – see if Kim fancied a sniff. Hey! I looked at my reflection. You're Jacqueline *Good*, right? I said. So how come *you're* getting these fun ideas all of a sudden? Learning from that *other* Jacqueline, are we?

Kim was sitting at a table slurping Coke when I walked in. The only other people were an old man whose dog was tied up outside, and Doris, wiping off her counter with a rag. 'Coke, please.' I looked across at Kim. 'Any crisps, Kim?'

Kim pulled a face and the old man growled, 'Crisps. Money to burn, kids today.'

Old Doris looked at him. 'Give up moaning,

Ken, you miserable so-and-so. *You* do all right –
twenty fags a day, sausage roll for the dog. Here
y'are love.' She slid the freezing can towards me,
took my coins and went on talking to Ken. 'If you
was *Selwyn* now, you'd have something to moan
about. Heard about the greenhouse, I suppose?'

The old guy nodded. 'Aye. Ruined. Years of
work. Kids, I reckon.' I sat down, pretending not
to be interested but earwigging like mad.

'Selwyn thinks not. There was a man – a tramp.
Asked Selwyn for his cap and got funny when he
wouldn't give it to him. Selwyn suspects *him*.'

I clamped my lips round my straw to keep
from grinning. Poor old Selwyn. Poor old *tramp*.
Still – it put *us* in the clear, didn't it? I looked
across at old Kim, decked out in leather jacket and
loose top over black jeans and the boots with pink
laces. 'Hey Kim,' I whispered. 'Fancy a radically
new experience?' I sounded like one of those
flipping car ads on the box.

28

Kim's sudden, yelping laugh made old Ken slop his tea.

'Ssssh!' I snatched back the bottle, corked it under the table and slipped it in my pocket. The old man fussed with a sodden tissue, muttering loudly about kids today till Doris came with her rag and mopped up the spillage.

I whispered, 'Funny feeling or what?'

Kim giggled. 'You can say *that* again. It's awesome. What the heck *is* it?'

'Dunno, but it's nice, isn't it? Makes you feel like doing something *seriously* out of line.'

'Does it do that to you, *too*?' Old Kim. She practically yelled it.

'Ssssh! Yes it *does*, but keep the noise down for Pete's sake.'

Ken drained his cup and got up, screeching his chair on the boards. 'I'll be off,' he grunted at Doris, 'somewhere I can get a bit of peace.'

We watched him shuffle through the doorway and bend to untie the old terrier which capered, yipping and fanning its tail as it tugged him out of sight. 'Old misery,' I growled.

'Hey!' I twisted round in my seat. Doris was glaring at me. 'Ken Partridge fought in France before you were born – before your *mother* was born for that matter, so we'll have a bit of respect if you don't mind.'

'OK. Sorry.' I turned back to Kim. 'Wait a minute, then go and ask for a toasted teacake.'

Kim giggled. 'Why?'

'You'll see. Just do it.'

She got up and went over to the counter. 'Toasted teacake, please.'

'Just the one?'

'Yeah.'

'It'll be a minute or two.' Doris waddled off into the poky galley where she did simple snacks.

I joined Kim at the counter. 'Open your bag.'

'What?'

92

'Your bag, turkey. Open it.'

Kim's shoulder bag matched her jacket. She unzipped it and I started helping myself from the cartons of choc bars, mints and packets of crisps on the counter. I worked quickly; scooping up handfuls, dropping them in the bag and going back for more, taking care not to leave any carton empty. By the time I heard the toaster pop, Kim's bag was almost full. 'Pay her and leave,' I hissed. 'It's forty pence. I'll be by the door.'

We crossed the park, passing close to the greenhouse, and found a knoll from which to watch poor Selwyn Tordoff as he came and went, clearing up as best he could. We sat munching our loot and laughing till the buzz wore off and we noticed how cold we were.

I was scared all day Monday. Not about the greenhouse. I told Craig and the others about the tramp and they loved it. No. It was the Pavilion. You see, the stuff in that bottle makes you brave, but it makes you *reckless* as well. You don't *think* before you do things. The thinking comes after, when it wears off, and what *I* was thinking was this. Old Doris didn't *see* us take the goodies, but she was bound to notice stuff was missing and who else *could* have taken them? I mean, suppose nobody else ordered anything cooked yesterday? It was quite possible. Most people just want coffee or tea or Coke. What if she never went in the galley after she toasted Kim's teacake – if that was the *one* time she couldn't see the counter? She'd remember that, wouldn't she? And she wouldn't need a university education to work out which school we were at. *That* was why I was scared. I mentioned it to Kim and it turned out *she* was having kittens too. 'It's all your fault,' she said. Charming.

Anyway, nothing happened, and by hometime we were both feeling a lot better. We walked home together and Kim asked where I got the bottle. I said London. Where in London? Ah, I said, that'd be telling. It made a nice change to have something she didn't have.

It didn't last, though, the good feeling. After dinner, Mum and me were drinking coffee while Dad hid behind the local rag. You could see the top of his head and his fingernails. Mum reckons it's rude to read at the table but Dad does it just the same. Anyway, he grunted and said, 'I don't know – makes you wonder what the world's coming to.'

Mum put her cup down. 'What's that, dear?'

'Park,' said Dad, sending my heart into my trainers. 'The greenhouse. Some tramp got in, Saturday night. Pulled up five hundred seedlings and replanted them upside down. Can you *believe* it? Killed the lot, of course. Then he ran off leaving the door wide open, and the frost killed all the tropical stuff as well.'

'Twisted, some people,' said Mum. 'They ought to lock him up and throw away the key, *if* they ever catch him, which I doubt.'

'Oh, they've *got* him,' said Dad. 'He was up in front of the magistrate this morning. Guilty.'

'I expect they'll find he's loony,' said Mum. 'You'd *have* to be loony to do a thing like that. Wants putting away for his own good.'

Loony. I didn't finish my coffee. I went up to my room and sat looking in the mirror. Was I loony? *Was* I? Maybe you *had* to be crazy to sniff something you found in the attic. Could you *tell* somebody was loony by the way they looked?

Did *sane* people talk to their reflections?

30

We got caught, Kim and me, next morning. Trubshaw brought old Doris into Maths, and there was a policewoman with them. It was the worst moment of my life. I knew the game was up. Trub murmured something to Mrs Birkby and she clapped her hands. 'Stop what you're doing, Year Six, and look this way. Do it *now*, Kim Farlow, not next week.' She turned to Doris. 'Do you see either of them here, Mrs Backhouse?'

Doris's eyes flicked from face to face. Mine was scarlet. I could feel it burning but there was nothing I could do. Her eyes stopped at me. 'That girl there – *she's* one of them.'

'Come out, Jacqueline Hyde.'

'But Miss, I . . .'

'COME OUT!'

'Yes, Miss.'

Doris scanned the faces till she found Kim. 'That's her. She's the other one.'

'Out here, Kim Farlow.'

Every eye followed as our little procession filed out. Trub in the lead, then me and Kim, then Doris and the policewoman.

'All right, Year Six,' sighed Mrs Birkby as the door was closing. 'Carry on.'

I didn't half wish I was back there, carrying on.

We had to wait in the secretary's office while Trub phoned our parents. The policewoman sat with us. The secretary knew we were in trouble and ignored us. I wanted to say something to Kim but you can't – not with somebody listening. I pictured Mum getting the call. She'd be distraught. She'd call Dad at the shop and *he* wouldn't be overjoyed either. I wished I'd never clapped eyes on that bottle. Or that I had it with me now, but it was in my bag in Mrs Birkby's room.

It was half an hour before they called us in. Mum and Dad were there, and Kim's folks, sitting in a row with Trub and old Doris. They looked like a treeful of owls. Trub asked if we'd anything to say. I couldn't think of anything. Kim said, 'We're sorry. We didn't know what we were doing. We'd sniffed something, you see.'

'*Sniffed* something?' The policewoman frowned. 'What sort of something?'

'Glue,' I broke in. 'It was some glue I got in London.'

Dad groaned, and the policewoman said, 'Where is it now, this glue?'

'I – chucked it away. In some bushes in the park.'

There were more questions. Where was the stuff we pinched. Had we sold it or shared it with anybody else. Had we hidden it somewhere. I don't think they believed we'd scoffed the lot. I thought they were going to send us to a detention centre or something, but Trub said Mrs Backhouse had decided not to press charges. I wished he'd told us that at the beginning.

We got a reprimand from the policewoman. That's a telling off, but if you think it's nothing you're dead wrong. They did it in the sick room. We had to go in separately, with our parents. Kim went first. You could hear the policewoman shouting through two doors. Kim came out crying. I thought, not me. You won't make *me* cry, but she did. She knew *exactly* the things to say. You know – stuff that *really* got to you. I broke down, I don't mind admitting it.

And the worst thing was, it didn't end there. No way. We had to finish out the school day, red-eyed and bedraggled. Everybody looking at us. Whispering. Even the teachers. Craig Lampton sneered in my face when he saw I'd been crying. We didn't know where to put ourselves. And when the buzzer finally went it only released us to go home, and who'd be waiting for us at home, eager to inflict further hassle?

Go on – have a guess.

'Sit down, Jacqueline.' Dad, the second I walked in. Him and Mum at the kitchen table, looking dead concerned.

'Can I hang my coat up, get rid of this bag?' Sarky, but polite as well.

Dad nodded, looking down at his hands. I went through to the hallway, draped my coat on the newel post and carried my bag upstairs. I'd have left it at the bottom but the bottle was inside. I wasn't going to *keep* it – not after this lot, but I didn't want *them* finding it.

'Now,' said Dad in a businesslike way as I sat down opposite him. Mum was to my left, at the end. Only my brother was missing. The shop, I mean. My brother the shop. 'What's going on, Jacqueline? Where's the quiet, clever girl you used to be? What's changed you? And what on *earth* possessed you to sniff *glue*, for heaven's sake?'

What the heck was I supposed to *say*? I shrugged, and Dad said, 'That's no answer, a shrug. *Something*'s changed you, and your mother and I want to know what. We're *entitled* to know.'

Entitled. I shook my head. 'I can't tell you, Dad, but it's over, I swear. There won't be anything else like this.' I was going to throw the bottle away, see? I'd decided.

Dad sighed. 'I hope you mean that, Jacqueline, because your mother's been frantic with worry.' He gazed at me. 'Has it just been the glue, or is there something else? Are you fretting about something? You know you can tell us *anything*, don't you, and we'll understand. Anything at all.'

Oh, sure. You know the greenhouse, Dad? All those seedlings? Well, *I* did that. Me and the Lampton gang. I'm a member, you see. And it *was* me on the school roof, and I flooded some wash-rooms in London as well, and what's more I loved every minute of it. How about *that*?

I didn't *say* this, of course. All I said was, 'There's nothing else. It was just the glue. I'll never sniff it again.'

'And the nightmares, Jacqueline?' said Mum. 'What about those?'

I shrugged. 'The glue, I guess. They won't come any more.'

'It's just . . . well, what you *told* me, Jacqueline, you know – about the old man and the girl in white?'

'Uh-huh?'

'Well . . . it reminded me of something. Something I read when I was about your age, so I phoned Grandma.'

'And?'

'Doctor Jekyll and Mr Hyde, Jacqueline. It's a story by Robert Louis Stevenson. There's a copy in Grandma's bookcase. Were you reading it when you were there, dear?'

'No.'

'Are you absolutely *sure*, Jacqueline?' She had a funny look on her face and I didn't know why. Not yet.

'Sure. I've heard of it, but I haven't read it.'

'Oh. Oh well . . . never mind, darling.' She wasn't looking too happy though and I thought to myself, I'll check it out, that story – see what she's on about.

And that was it. End of interview. Jacqueline promises to be good so Mummy and Daddy can concentrate on their favourite child again.

Isn't that nice?

32

I did it Wednesday morning, very early. Got rid of the bottle. Six o'clock. Nobody stirs before seven at our house. I locked myself in the bathroom and emptied the stuff down the lavatory. It took a while because it was treacly, and all the time I could feel Jacqueline Bad trying to stop me. Whispering in my head. I hummed a tune so I wouldn't hear.

I didn't flush the lavatory. I'd need that noise to drown my footsteps when I went downstairs. I turned on the cold tap and ran water into the bottle. When it was half full I shook it as if I was rinsing out a milk bottle and tipped the froth down the plughole. I did this twice then tiptoed back to my room, keeping the bottle away from my nose just in case. I got into some jeans and a jumper, shoved the bottle in my pocket and crept back to the bathroom. It was seven minutes past six. No sound came from Mum and Dad's room. I flushed the lavatory, scuttled down the stairs and let myself out through the front door.

Four doors down some new people were moving in. They weren't up yet of course, but a skip stood by their gateway, piled high with rubbish. I'd noticed it yesterday. I glanced both ways. Nobody about. I walked along to the skip and lobbed the bottle on top. There was a clink, and that was that.

I hurried back, rinsed my hands at the kitchen sink and crept upstairs. The cistern was still filling. My parents hadn't stirred. I undressed and got into bed. Some time today guys would come for the skip. Its contents would end up in a landfill somewhere, and there, under tons of rubbish, the bottle would be lost for ever. I smiled, though a part of me was sad. 'So long, Jacqueline Bad,' I whispered. There was no answer, but I swear that as I rolled over and pulled up the duvet, I heard a distant laugh.

33

I know what you're thinking. You're thinking, she chucked the bottle away so how come she ends up *here*, talking to me? That should've been the end of it, right?

Wrong.

It was OK for a while, if you don't count that I had no friends any more. Craig Lampton sacked me for crying, and Kim was giving me the chill because her folks stopped her clothes allowance. As though it was *my* flipping fault. And anyway, she had enough clothes already to see her through the next Ice Age. Oh, and the teachers were pretty mean, too. I was Jacqueline Good again, right? Their favourite, but you wouldn't know it. They never let their faces slip. Watching me all the time, picking on me. Talk about give a dog a bad name.

It wasn't a million laughs at home, either. I had to come straight home after school – not that there was anywhere *else* to go – and I wasn't allowed out evenings or weekends except with Mum. You'd think I'd murdered somebody.

But the worst bit was that the dreams didn't stop. The nightmares. They didn't come *every* night, but when they did, they were every bit as horrible as before. In my dreams I was forever running, forever hiding, forever afraid. And no matter how fast I ran or how well I hid, the girl in white always found me. Her eyes, like the eyes of God, were everywhere.

I still blamed the bottle. I thought, if I hang on, the dreams will go away. If I hadn't believed that, I think I'd have cracked up completely.

This went on all through November, and then in December something happened that scared me half to death. No, I *don't* want to talk about it. Not really.

I *wish* you'd stop tapping your teeth with your pencil like that.

34

At school, the approach of Christmas sparked off the usual frenzy of activity. The timetable was abandoned, sport and club sessions were suspended and teachers competed for hall time, piano time and crepe paper. Old Trubshaw called it Collapsing into Christmas, and it seemed to start a week earlier every year.

My year was rehearsing group and individual presentations for the concert in just under three weeks' time. Parents would attend the concert, and Governors, and possibly the Mayor of Wexham, and the local press might send a reporter. It was a big date on the school calendar and everything had to be spot on.

Everybody in Year Six was doing something except me. If you weren't in one of the groups getting up playlets or sketches, you were supposed to choose something to do solo – a tune if you played an instrument, or a song, or a poem, or a conjuring trick if that was your thing. Like I said, I wasn't exactly flavour of the month right then. Nobody had invited me to join their group and I hadn't thought up a solo act because I couldn't be bothered. The nightmares were doing my head in if you must know. I was totally knackered all the time. I just didn't *feel* Christmassy. I thought if I hung around rehearsals and kept quiet, maybe nobody'd notice.

I was wrong though. One Thursday afternoon, Old Nitwit sent for me. He was concert co-ordinator.

'Now, Jacqueline,' he said, eyeballing me across his cluttered desk. 'I don't seem to have you down for anything in the concert. Whose group are you in?'

'Nobody's, sir.'

'So it's to be a solo performance, eh?' He smiled. 'Brave girl. What're you thinking of doing?'

'Nothing, sir.'

His smile faded. 'What d'you mean, nothing? Everybody has to do something, you know that. What's the matter – don't you *like* Christmas?'

'It's OK, sir, but I don't *feel* Christmassy this year.' To be perfectly honest I was nearly crying.

'You don't feel *Christmassy*? Why not, Jacqueline? Are you ill?'

'I don't know, sir. I think I might be . . . sort of.'

'Well – do your parents know, Jacqueline? Have you seen the doctor?'

'No, sir. It's not that sort of illness. It's . . . in my head, sir. In my mind.'

'Hmmm.' He clasped his hands on the desktop and looked at them, the wally. 'And what form does this . . . illness take, Jacqueline?'

'How d'you mean, sir?'

'Well – what *happens*, girl? Do you vomit, shake, collapse – what?'

'I have dreams, sir. Nightmares.'

'*Everybody* has nightmares, Jacqueline. Doesn't mean they're ill.'

'Mine are always the same, sir.'

He nodded. 'Recurring nightmares. Lots of people get those, too.'

'I don't sleep, sir. I'm tired all the time. I can't be bothered *doing* anything.'

111

'We all feel like that at times, Jacqueline.' I might as well have been talking to a bison. 'We all go through bad patches. The secret is not to give in to them.' He gave me the smile again. 'Come on – snap out of it. You're young. You've got a good home and the use of all your limbs. You're not blind or hungry or homeless. Count your blessings, child. *Smile.*' He opened a drawer. 'Look – there's a poem here I've been *dying* to squeeze into the concert.' He held up a book. '*A Visit From St Nicholas*, by Clement Clark Moore. Heard of it?'

'No, sir.'

'*What?*' He leafed through the book. 'One of the finest Christmas poems ever written. I thought *everybody* knew it. Listen. *'Twas the night before Christmas, when all through the house . . .*'

'Oh, *that* one.' I nodded. 'I've heard it, sir, but I didn't know what it was called.'

'Well, you do now, and I'd like you to recite it at the concert.'

I went cold. 'I . . . I *can't*, sir. Not *that* one.'

'Oh? Why not, Jacqueline? Why *not* this one?'

'It's a *kid's* poem, sir. Santa Claus. I don't *believe* in Santa Claus and neither do any of the others. They'd all laugh at me, sir.'

'Nonsense, child. It's a lovely, traditional Christmas poem. The parents will remember it from *their* schooldays, and so will the Mayor. They'll love it. Nobody will laugh at you, you silly girl.'

'The kids will.' I was crying. I couldn't help it. 'They don't like me as it *is*. If I have to say that poem, they'll kill themselves laughing.'

'Rubbish!' He slid the book across the desk and stood up. 'Everybody joins in the Christmas concert, Jacqueline. *Everybody*. Now pull yourself together, take that poem and learn it. I'll see you next week, when I shall expect you to be word perfect. That's all, Jacqueline. Off you go.'

A star, old Nitwit. A prince among men.

35

The concert was scheduled for the evening of Tuesday, December 19th – the day before school broke up for Christmas. On Monday the 18th in the afternoon, there was a full dress rehearsal. I knew the rotten poem and hated it. Nitwit had me down to perform between two group productions – a playlet set in World War One called *Christmas in the Trenches*, and a humorous sketch about dinner ladies. Another class were on first and I was sitting with our lot in the audience. We weren't watching though. Most of us were messing about – passing notes and telling mucky jokes and giggling. *I* wasn't – I was being ostracized as usual, plus I was dead nervous about

114

reciting that cretinous poem. For the first time since getting rid of it, I wished I had the bottle. I thought, Jacqueline *Bad* wouldn't stand up there bleating rubbish like this. I had this crumpled printout I'd been learning from and what I was doing was, I was scribbling alternative lines in the margin, turning it into a poem about vampires. It was better than the original, though I say it myself. Anyway, I was so wrapped up in what I was doing that before I knew it, it was my turn.

I made up a few more lines waiting backstage, but I couldn't really concentrate by then. The dreaded moment was at hand, and I knew only too well what was about to happen.

Anthony Netherwood spoke the closing lines of *Christmas in the Trenches*. As the applause faded, Mr Whittaker cleared his throat and strode onto the stage. 'And now, ladies and gentlemen, Year Six proudly presents Miss Jacqueline Hyde, who will recite for us *A Visit From St Nicholas*.'

I hissed, 'Creepazoid' as I passed him in the wings. I didn't know whether he heard or not and I didn't care. Disaster was waiting for me out there and it was all his fault.

'A Visit From St Nicholas, by Clement Clark Moore.' I felt my cheeks burn and my voice sort of wavered. I fixed my eyes on a high window at the back of the hall and waded in.

'*'Twas the night before Christmas, when all through the house*
Not a creature was stirring, not even a ...'

'BRONTOSAURUS!' yelled Craig Lampton, and the kids cracked up laughing. I tried to carry on.

'*... mouse.*
The stockings were hung by the chimney with ...'

'SAUSAGES!' cried Mary-Beth Summerscales. Screams of laughter from the rotten audience. I had to gulp and bite my lip to keep from crying. Don't cry, I told myself. If you burst out crying now, in front of the whole school, you might as well be dead. I couldn't continue though. No way. I was about to run offstage when old Trubshaw strode on with a face like thunder. You should've heard that laughter stop, like someone had cut it with a knife. Kids shifted in their seats and looked at the floor. Trub glared down.

Give him his due, he *really* laid into them.

'Never before,' he said in this really quiet voice, 'in twenty-two years as a teacher, have I witnessed such rudeness as you people have exhibited just now.' He paused, while his eyes raked the rows of faces like a machine-gun. You could've heard a pin drop in that pause. 'I see that some of you have at least the grace to blush, and I'm glad of that. *I* blush. For the first time in my life, I'm *ashamed* to be associated with my school. Ashamed that such behaviour should be possible in persons under my care.'

There was more. As Trub socked it to 'em, Nitwit crept on and steered me off. I didn't say anything, but if looks could kill he'd have died right there in the wings, the plonker. I thought, well at least it's over. I've proved my point. I won't have to do it on the night.

Boy, was I wrong! D'you know what he *did*? He patted me on the shoulder and said in this brisk voice, 'It'll be all right tomorrow, Jacqueline – nobody'll *dare* laugh now.'

36

'Mum?'

'Yes, dear?'

'You and Dad – you won't be coming to the concert tomorrow night, will you?'

'Oh, Jacqueline – you *know* how busy it gets in the shop around Christmas. And besides, I don't think we'd dare show our faces this year, after that embarrassing business with the police. You should start thinking about what you want to pack for Grandma's.'

'Do I *have* to go to Grandma's, Mum? I'm eleven. I could easily stay here while you and Dad see to the shop.'

'Well, dear – if we thought we could trust you

to behave sensibly then perhaps you *could* stay, but we don't. Not after that . . .'

'Embarrassing business with the police,' I finished for her. 'You're never going to let me forget that, are you, Mum?'

'Not till I'm sure you've come to your senses. You used to be such a *good* girl, Jacqueline. Everybody said so.'

'I know.' Yes, and where did it get me? Put upon, that's where. Taken advantage of. Oh, *Jacqueline*'ll do it. You don't mind, do you dear? Yuk!

After tea I locked myself in my room as usual. I was getting more and more like the guy I became in my nightmare – locking myself away, avoiding people. I lay on the bed thinking, but *not* about what I wanted to pack for Grandma's. I couldn't even *begin* to think about anything else till tomorrow was over. That poem. I couldn't believe old Nitwit had *said* what he did. Nobody'll *dare* laugh now. Probably not, but was that the point? If people didn't *want* the rotten poem – if they had to be *frightened* into sitting through it, why leave it in? Why should *I* stand up in front of all those people and recite a poem I hated and they didn't want to listen to?

119

Maybe I'd chuck a sickie. Tell Mum I'd got the bellyache. With a bit of luck I could make it last through Wednesday, then there'd be no more school till January when old Whittaker would have forgotten all about the stupid concert.

No. Mum wouldn't fall for it. She never did. I'd just have to *do* it, wouldn't I? Oh, where were you, Jacqueline Bad, now that I needed you?

37

Do I *have* to go into this? *Do* I? It scares me, the bit where I'm not in control any more. I mean OK, I loved the buzz. I'm not denying it. I loved it every time but you see, I got to say *when*. I chose the time and place and who I was with and all that, but *this* time – the time you want me to tell about – I didn't. Yes, I *know* that's why I'm here. I'm not stupid, but it scares me and I don't like to talk about it.

OK, OK – you win. You always win.

Well, first I want to say it wasn't planned – leastwise not by *me*. Yes, I *know* I scribbled those words in the margin. Those alternative verses, but I was passing the time, that's all. I wasn't going to *say* them for Pete's sake – I was Jacqueline *Good*, remember? I'd *die* before I'd do what I did in front of the Mayor and everybody. It happened, that's all. It just *happened*. One moment I was hovering in the wings feeling scared and sick as Nitwit announced me, and the next I was standing tall in the footlights' glare, filled with that fierce joy I'd expected never to feel again.

'A Visit From St Nicholas, by Clement Clark Moore.' My voice was firm, confident. I didn't give a toss. It was the most wonderful feeling in the world.

' *'Twas the night before Christmas, and all through the tomb*
Not a creature was stirring – there wasn't much room.'

There was a sort of rustling in the audience. You could practically *hear* the wrinklies asking themselves, does it *really* begin like that – I'd forgotten.

'The stockings were hung by the chimney – and look,
The legs in them bled on the carpet – ooh, yuk!'

Somebody tittered, then it dawned on the audience that I was doing a skit – that it was OK to laugh, and they did. And this time they were laughing *with* me, not *at* me. My heart soared.

'The vampires were snuggling all warm in their beds,
With visions of jugular veins in their heads;
And Ma in the belfry and I in the crypt
Were dreaming of victims whose blood we had sipped,
When out on the lawn Peter Cushing appeared
With a stake and a torch and the cross we all feared.
Away to the window I flew . . .'

It went on like that. I don't know how I *managed* it – I didn't have the words with me and I'd made no effort to memorize them. They just came out. And the audience *loved* it. They did. You should've heard the cheering at the end, the applause. I bet the Mayor himself was cheering. I bowed and exited, grinning and waving and feeling ten feet tall and the applause continued, even when I'd gone.

It wasn't till I was sipping Coke in the makeshift dressing room with Mary-Beth Summerscales pounding my back that it hit me. I choked on my drink and went cold. Jacqueline Bad was back, and I hadn't sniffed that bottle in months.

38

While I was changing, Trub phoned Dad. I suspect Nitwit put him up to it. I don't know what he said exactly, but he must've made it seem like I'd sabotaged the entire concert and made a laughing stock of his school. I didn't know this at the time. All that happened was that Nitwit stuck his head round the door and told me the Head would want to see me in the morning, which was no big surprise. It was when I got home that the fertilizer hit the revolving blades.

I won't bang on about it except to say it was awful. Really awful. You'd have thought I was a serial killer the way they looked at me when I walked in. I was a disgrace, they said. An embarrassment. I'd shamed them, betrayed my teachers and damaged the school. Thank goodness they hadn't been there. It went on and on. They kept asking me to explain and of course I couldn't, not without mentioning the bottle, but they kept nagging away till they wore me down and I *did* mention it.

They didn't believe me, of course. Kept going on about *glue*. I'd been sniffing glue. I'd admitted as much the other week, during that embarrassing business with the police. Why was I trying to pretend now that it was something else?

I wished I'd kept the bottle. Emptied it, rinsed it out and kept it. They'd have *had* to believe me then. I was scared, see? Scared of what had happened to me that night. I needed help not hassle, but I wasn't going to get it while my parents thought I was lying to them.

It was then I remembered the cork. I'd uncorked the bottle in the bathroom and dropped the cork in the pocket of my dressing gown. I'd come across it a couple of days later, transferred it to my drawer and promptly forgotten about it. I looked at them across the table. 'I . . . I've remembered something. In my room. Can I go get it?'

It took a bit of finding, but I located it in a corner and took it downstairs. They sniffed it, handled it, held it up to the light. 'Hmmm,' went Dad. 'It's pretty old, but it might have come from anywhere. What d'you think, Sandra?'

Mum shook her head and looked at me. 'This bottle. You say you found it in the old cabinet in Grandma's attic?'

'Yes, in one of the drawers.'

'Only it's odd, because that cabinet's been there as far back as I can remember. I'd have thought if there was anything in it, it'd have been found long ago.'

What was I supposed to say? I shrugged. 'The bottle was there, Mum. I wish it hadn't been, but it was.' It was half past ten and I was washed out.

Mum looked at her watch. 'Bit late to phone Grandma now. I'll do it in the morning – see what *she* thinks.' She looked at me. 'You'd better get off to bed, young woman. School tomorrow.'

It turned out they'd be coming with me. To school I mean. Trub had asked to see them, but they hadn't bothered mentioning it to me till that minute. Maybe they thought it rounded things off nicely. Thanks a lot, I thought, dragging

39

I got Pindown. That's what the kids call it. Officially it's Monitored Probation, or M.P. It's a last resort before they expel you, and of course nobody expected it to happen to Jacqueline Hyde.

Trub was *dead* mad about my poem. I was gobsmacked. I thought at least he'd admit everybody loved it. I expected *some* punishment for what I'd done, but *not* Pindown.

What happens is, you get a journal. It's just an exercise book but they call it a journal, and every day you, your teachers and your parents have to write in it. Your teachers put how you've worked in their class and what your behaviour's been like

129

and all that. Your parents sign to say you've done the task you've been set for the evening – kids on M.P. have a task *every* evening, and weekends too and *you* write how *you* think you've done that day. This goes on for a term. A whole flipping *term*, and it's even more of a drag than it sounds. You're watched, you see. Every minute. It's like being at school twenty-four hours a day. And you can't put *I was fantastic today* if it isn't true, because your teachers and parents read what you've put, and if you haven't been honest you get what they call a demerit. You get a demerit for each bad comment by a teacher or parent as well, and if you get six demerits in the term, you're out.

Oh, and part of the deal is that your parents have to deliver you to school every morning and collect you every afternoon. You can't leave the building till a teacher hands over your journal. You can imagine how delighted Dad was at the prospect of having to do this five days a week for thirteen weeks. We've only one car, so it meant he wouldn't get to the shop till twenty past nine at the earliest, and he'd have to close early, too.

All this was to start on day one of the new term in January, so now I had *two* terrific things to look forward to – Grandma's for Christmas and Pindown in the New Year.

And it wasn't my fault. It wasn't *me*. It was Jacqueline Bad. Could *I* help it if she decided to take over from time to time?

Oh-oh – *that's* got you writing in your little book again, hasn't it? What're you putting? *This girl's seriously crackers*? Or do shrinks not say that?

What am I *doing* spilling my guts to a psychiatrist anyway?

40

It was cold and wet when we got to Grandma's house on Friday lunchtime. There's this annual ritual where Grandma takes me up to my room while Mum and Dad smuggle in my Christmas presents and hide them. I'm not supposed to know what's going on but I'm *eleven* for Pete's sake. Anyway, it happened same as always and I didn't say anything. I suppose I was lucky there *were* presents after all the hassle I'd caused.

It was still raining at half past two when Mum and Dad left. I stood on the doorstep and waved them off, wondering what Mum had said on the phone yesterday and whether Grandma would mention it.

She didn't. She went off to do the dishes and I wandered into the front room and stood gazing through the window. The trees were leafless in the square across the street. The street itself gleamed dully under a leaden sky and green iron railings dripped depressingly. It'll be like this the whole fortnight, I told myself. It always is.

I pictured the Volvo swishing down the M4. Mum and Dad chatting, relieved to be rid of me. Two weeks with nobody but their favourite kid to think about. The shop.

I left the window and trailed about the room, looking at Grandma's sad stuff. Dark, heavy furniture. Trinkets and vases. Faded prints in tarnished frames: children, dogs, Monarch of the Glen. In the farthest corner stood a tall bookcase with leaded glass doors; its shelves crammed with old, leatherbound volumes which she never took down except to dust. For something to do I began reading their titles, starting on the top shelf. *The Last Days of Pompeii. What a Young Wife Should Know. The Rose and the Ring. The Man-Eating Tigers of Rudraprayag. Sometime Never. The Cloister and the Hearth. Dr Jekyll and Mr Hyde.*

Dr Jekyll and Mr Hyde. That was the book Mum asked me about, wasn't it? The one I decided to check out? Well, OK – I'd nothing better to do. I reached up, pulled it out and flicked through its fusty, foxed pages. There was only one picture – an engraved frontispiece showing a man in what looked like a laboratory. The man's head was flung back, his tongue protruded and he was clutching his throat. A flask he'd been holding had slipped from his hand and was falling.

I sat down on the sofa and read the first bit. *Mr Utterson the lawyer was a man of rugged countenance* . . . Boring start. Give it a chance though, eh? It had someone called Hyde in it and you could never tell – it might pick up as I got into it.

probably know what it is 'cause I bet you've read the story. Anyway, it turns out this guy Hyde is the bad side of a doctor called Jekyll. That's why the story's called Doctor Jekyll and Mr Hyde. See – this doctor's a really *good* guy. Everybody *respects* him, you know? He's like a pillar of society, right? Then he invents this stuff – this *potion* – which he drinks and it turns him into Mr Hyde, who isn't good at all. In fact, he's evil. He goes round at night doing evil things, but it's OK 'cause he can drink this *other* stuff and turn back into Doctor Jekyll.

Then something goes wrong, because he starts turning into Mr Hyde when he doesn't want to – when he hasn't drunk the potion. Is all this *reminding* you of something? I thought it might. It reminded *me*, I can tell you. I was scared stiff, especially at the end where the doctor realizes there's no way out and kills himself with poison.

Oh, I tried to find a rational explanation. Told myself I must've read the story when I was little and forgotten it, apart from in my whatsit – subconscious. I thought, when I'm asleep my subconscious plays back the story like a video in my head, and in this video I play Mr Hyde. Sounds reasonable, right? But then what about the bottle? I didn't dream *that*. And the stuff I did after sniffing. That was *real*.

And Jacqueline Bad, taking over at the concert when I hadn't sniffed in weeks.

Like I said, I was scared stiff. I sat there on the sofa for ages with the book in my lap, staring at nothing. It was getting dark outside but I didn't notice. Then Grandma came in and switched on the light and said, 'Jacqueline?' and I burst into tears.

They should've brought me here *then*. If they had, that lovely belt would be round someone's middle and I wouldn't have done the school but it's always too late, isn't it?

42

She cuddled me like a baby while I cried. I wanted to talk. I had to tell someone what was happening to me. How scared I was, but I couldn't stop crying. It was like all the stuff I'd kept corked up inside was coming out. My loneliness. The feeling that Mum and Dad didn't really want me. My suspicion that I might be going mad. I'm not kidding – it must've been at least ten minutes before I got enough control to speak, and when I did, I told her everything. Finding the bottle. That first sniff, and the feeling it gave me of being alive – *really* alive for the first time in my life. I told how I sneered at my reflection in the mirror – how suddenly I despised Jacqueline Good and all that she stood for, which was why I hurled the flatiron. I said I realized then that I was *two* people – Jacqueline Good and Jacqueline Bad, and that of the two I preferred Jacqueline Bad. I told how I smuggled the bottle home and used it to summon my bad half, and the things I'd done as Jacqueline Bad. I mentioned my nightmares – how they were identical to incidents in the story I'd just read, and I told about the poor homeless guy who'd gone to jail. I described my police reprimand and throwing the bottle away. And finally I got to the concert, and how Jacqueline Bad had taken over without my wanting her to and how terrified I'd been ever since, wondering when she'd do it again.

When it stopped pouring out of me she didn't say anything. Not at first. I suppose she was thinking. My head was on her chest and she was stroking my hair. I nearly fell asleep, it was such a relief to have told someone. The problem hadn't gone away – I'm not saying that, but it felt like the *pressure* was released, if that makes sense.

After a bit she said, 'And you're absolutely *sure* you've never read that story till just now, Jacqueline?'

I nodded. My tears had made a damp patch on her blouse.

'What about the film? There's a film. Could you have watched it on TV, d'you think?'

'No. I'd remember.' I sat up and looked at her. 'That Doctor Jekyll – could he have lived here, Grandma? In this house?'

She smiled and shook her head. 'Doctor Jekyll never lived *anywhere*, darling – he's a fictional character.'

'Are you *sure*? That stuff . . . the stuff in the bottle. I think it must've been the potion. Why *else* would I dream a story I've never read?'

She shook her head. 'I don't know, Jacqueline. It's a mystery.' She smiled, dabbing my cheek with a Kleenex. 'The world's full of mysteries, you know, and we'll never solve them all. What *you've* got to do is put all of this behind you. I know you're afraid of Jacqueline Bad, but I'll tell you what *I* think. I think now you've made up your mind to leave her behind she'll fade away, together with the nightmares. You'll see – a few quiet days with Grandma and you'll be your old self again.'

Sounds good, eh? It did to me at that moment. I went to bed and had the best night's sleep I'd

had in weeks, but that wasn't the end of it. Well
– being two people's an illness, isn't it? It's got a
name, and if it could be cured by a few quiet days
with Grandma you'd be able to get grandmas on
the National Health.

Next day, Saturday, I took it easy. Well – I'd slept OK. No dream that I could remember, and certainly no nightmare. I thought, maybe Grandma's right. Maybe it *is* fading away. The next day was Christmas Eve. Nice to have it over and done with just in time for the day of days.

Sunday morning I felt great. It was a bit nippy but the sun was out. Grandma was baking for the next day. Mince pies. When I was little I used to enjoy helping her but not now, so I said, 'Think I'll take a stroll along the canal, Grandma. Check out the market.' That's the market I mentioned before, remember? The one with the washrooms?

It'd been closed last time because it was a weekday, but it'd be open today.

'It'll be frightfully busy, darling – Christmas Eve and all that.'

'I don't mind.'

'That's all right then.' She smiled. 'It's good to see you looking cheerful.'

I wrapped up warm and motored on down to the towpath. The water was dark with the reflections of tall buildings on the far bank, mostly abandoned. There were quite a few people about. Kids. Dog walkers. A jogger. The closer I got to the market, the more people there were.

Grandma was right. It *was* busy. I left the towpath and joined the crowds pushing and shoving between stalls. There was some good stuff: T-shirts, jackets, belts. There was jewellery too, and candles and posters and perfumed oils and decorations made with dried flowers, as well as the usual festive stuff, but the best was the leather.

There was this railful of belts. *Gorgeous* belts with patterns of studs and chunky gothic buckles. I stopped to drool, lifting them to feel their weight, tracing their embossed designs with my fingers. Each belt had a price tag. I flipped one up.

Nineteen ninety-nine. *What*? Twenty quid for a flipping *belt*? You'd get the same thing for a fiver in Wexham, if they *had* stuff like this in Wexham, which they don't. It was a nice one – thick and wide with an antique-finish witch's head buckle, and I suddenly thought how terrific it'd look with Kim's leather jacket. I smiled, picturing her face if I came up to her in the schoolyard and said, 'There y'go Kim – I picked this up for you down Camden – thought it'd go with that jacket of yours.' She'd be chuffed to little mint balls. Might even be friends like before. Pity I had no dosh.

I don't know what happened next. Well, yes I *do*, but I don't know *how* it happened. Didn't feel it coming on or anything. One second I was stroking the belt, and the next I was pulling it off the rail, coiling it cool as you please and shoving it in my jeans pocket. The stallholder was up the far end showing earrings to two women, and the space between was full of jostling shoppers. Nobody noticed, or if they did, they didn't care. *I* didn't care either, I just walked on, dead cool, with this big bulge in my jeans.

I was back on the towpath when I realized I'd had another visit from my friend. It was a bad moment, I can tell you. My worst fears confirmed, as they say. I felt sick. Had to sit on a wall. I thought, bet I dream tonight.

I don't know how long I sat. Long time. People passing. Nobody asked was I OK or anything. Didn't even glance my way. Eventually it dawned on me I was shivering with cold as well as fear, so I stood up and walked on. I could feel the belt with every step. I didn't want it any more. Wished I'd never set eyes on it. I even thought about taking it back. Not owning *up* – I'm not *that* daft – putting it back on the rail. I didn't, though. What I did was, I waited till nobody was in sight, then chucked it in the canal. It uncoiled in the air like a snake and as soon as it hit the water, the weight of the buckle took it down. A line of little silver bubbles came up, and that was that.

I didn't tell Grandma. What was the point? If it got out I'd been naughty, Santa might not come.

Christmas Day was nice. I woke up at eight o'clock. I'd been dreaming: a weird, mixed-up dream, not too scary. I couldn't remember most of it. I got up and went downstairs and Santa *had* been.

Don't think I can't see you, eyeing me over the top of your pad. I know what you're thinking. You're thinking, does she believe in *Santa Claus*? At *eleven*? Well, no, I don't, so there. My presents were under the tree 'cause Grandma put them there before she went to bed, same as always. You can write *that* on your pad if you like.

I'd brought her present down with me. It was

a book about life in the Forties. All photos. Grandma was young in the Forties and enjoys remembering. I put the package under the tree and went out to the kitchen to put the kettle on. The whole thing's like *tradition*, you know? Her leaving my presents out after I'm in bed. Me getting up first, putting her gift under the tree and waking her with a cuppa. I never start opening my presents till she comes down. We like to ooh! and ahh! over each other's stuff. I got a walkman from Mum and Dad, some CDs and money for clothes.

After breakfast we went to church. We always do that, too. Grandma's been a regular attender since Grandad died, but Mum and Dad aren't churchgoers and I only go this one time each year. It's a nice church considering it's in the middle of town, and the vicar's nice as well. He's called Nicholas Cribb, which is a perfect Christmas name if you think about it. His sermon was about kings and shepherds. He said they're equal in God's eyes, then he smiled and said that went for queens and shepherdesses too, and then we sang a carol. It was lovely, the church all trimmed up with the crib out front and the sun through stained glass and the smell of candles. I even managed to forget about Jacqueline Bad for an hour. In fact, I don't think she was there.

We shook hands with the vicar, then strolled home in the watery sunshine to Christmas dinner. Just the two of us stuffing our faces, pulling crackers and wearing silly hats. Me trying not to think about my bad half, Grandma trying not to miss Grandad too much. At two o'clock Mum phoned, same as every year, and after that it was the Queen's message and a quiet evening in front of the telly.

OK, so it was nothing special. Millions were doing exactly the same all over the country, but that's what I liked about it. It was *normal*. I was an ordinary kid, enjoying an ordinary Christmas in an ordinary house.

I can't tell you how much I wish I was there right now.

Mum and Dad came for me on Monday, January 1st. Nothing drastic had happened in the week since Christmas Day – no more dreams, no more visits from my friend J.B. I wasn't letting my guard down, though. No way. She'll be back, I told myself, hoping I was wrong.

The new term would begin on Wednesday. I was dreading it. In fact it'd spoiled my week, thinking about it. Pindown. Thirteen weeks of relentless supervision. What would happen if my bad half decided to pay me a visit in the meantime? I'd get *another* term, wouldn't I? Or be expelled. And what were the chances of her *not* coming? Slim, I reckoned.

We all had lunch, then it was hugs and kisses all round and into the trusty Volvo, waving to Grandma through a haze of blue, brain-rotting exhaust. Dad looked at me in the mirror. 'Grandma tells us you've been fine, Jacqueline. No trouble at all.'

I shrugged and nodded. Well – what can you say?

'Daddy and I hope *very* much that you've turned over a new leaf, darling,' said Mum. 'We've been awfully worried, you know.'

'I know.' Not half as worried as I have, I thought. A new leaf'd be fine, but it wasn't up to me, was it? I didn't have control.

It was nice to be back in my own bed, but it was ages before I slept. I kept thinking about the belt at the bottom of the canal and the bottle under the rubbish. You can hide things but they're still *there*, aren't they? And of course I thought about school. How unfair it was that I couldn't *choose* to be good. I mean, I might decide to be an absolute *angel*, but if J.B. showed up, even on the last day of term, it would all have been for nothing.

Surely there was *something* I could do to help

myself, I thought, and of course there was. What d'you mean, *tell* me about it? You *know* about it. Yes, OK, OK. Pencil ready? Here we go.

46

Tuesday, January 2nd, 1996. The day I blew it.

It started innocently enough. I slept in because of fretting half the night, and when I looked out the bedroom window there was snow on the ground. Not a lot. Just enough to hide the soggy winter grass and make the trees look nice. I thought, pity it isn't six feet deep and still snowing so they can't open the school tomorrow.

Anyway, it was enough of a novelty to lure me out straight after breakfast. I'd bought these brilliant boots with some of my Christmas money – loose-fitting, soft black leather, mid-calf, turned down all round. Made in Italy. I couldn't wait to wear them – you can't buy boots like those in

Wexham. I thought I'd call for Kim. If she was speaking to me we could help each other make the most of our last day of freedom, *and* she'd see the boots.

She wasn't in. Nobody was. I bet her folks had taken her shopping – six stunning outfits for the new school year.

I wasn't ready to go home, so I motored along with my hands in my jacket pockets feeling cool in my London footwear. I wasn't headed anywhere in particular, so it was by chance that I found myself passing the school. At least I *thought* it was chance at the time. Now I'm not so sure. Somebody had already been there that morning – there were tyre tracks curving through the gateway, but there was no vehicle in the yard and no sign of anyone. For something to do I turned in and followed the tracks.

They stopped by the kitchen door, so there'd probably been a delivery of some sort. Spuds, I suppose. There were footprints and scuffmarks and you could see where the vehicle had reversed in a short arc, then shot back down the driveway.

I started walking round the building, looking in windows. Don't ask me why. I suppose Jacqueline Bad was in the process of taking over but I didn't notice. As far as I was concerned I was just killing time. Anyway, I went right round, and just before the last corner I saw that the window of the caretaker's little store room was open. The caretaker had probably come into school to take delivery of the spuds, and had gone in the store room for a crafty drag. Smoking was strictly prohibited in all parts of the school building except the staffroom and Trub's office, but it was common knowledge that the caretaker smoked in his store, with the window open to get rid of the smell. He'd probably been smoking when he heard the van, and by the time he'd finished seeing to the spuds he'd forgotten the window.

I stood gazing at it while a few things came together in my head. Smoking. Risk of fire. School tomorrow. Pindown. Big fire – no school. No school – no Pindown. Caretaker's fault – Jacqueline in the clear.

Don't look at me like that. It wasn't *me*, you see. It was her.

The store room's round the back of the school, so there was nobody to see me climb in. It was a bit dim inside but of course I didn't put the light on. I wasn't *that* daft.

He'd been careless. Left a cigarette end crushed out in the tin lid he used as an ashtray. Actually it was more than an end – nearly half a ciggy so the spudman must've caught him in mid smoke.

I straightened it out and looked for matches. Three warehouse coats were hanging behind the door. In a pocket of one of them was a disposable lighter. I tried it and it worked.

I rooted round and found some greasy old polishing cloths, a newspaper and some white spirit in a plastic container. I unscrewed the cap of the container and poured a quantity of spirit into the pocket in which I'd found the lighter. Then I placed the cloths and the newspaper on the floor directly under the warehouse coats. Spirit dripped onto them from the pocket.

I put the ciggy between my lips, snapped the lighter and lit up. I took a couple of drags to make sure it was going properly, then dropped it in the soggy pocket which flared up at once. A stream of tiny blue flames fell on the cloths and paper. They looked so pretty falling I'd have liked to stay and watch but it was time to go. I dropped the lighter in the disintegrating pocket and backed towards the window.

Outside, I didn't head for the driveway where

47

And of course it was the boots that got me caught. Footprints in the snow, all the way from the back of the half-gutted building to our side door. Like I said, you can't buy boots like those in Wexham.

If it hadn't snowed, there would have been no way they'd have found out it was me. On the other hand, if there'd been no snow I might not have taken that walk, or if I had, there'd have been no tyretracks for me to follow up the driveway. If, if, if . . .

I know what you're thinking. You're saying to yourself, what a plonker, not realizing she was leaving footprints. Well, I've thought about that, and I've come to the conclusion that I might have left that trail deliberately. Sounds daft? I don't think so. See – I was scared. Desperate. I was getting the nightmares and the visits from J.B. – what you call *flashbacks* here. I had no way of knowing what she might drive me to next. I needed help, but all I was getting was disbelief. Disbelief and Pindown. I don't *know* I left the footprints on purpose. I'm not saying that, but I wouldn't be *surprised*, that's all.

Anyway, if that *was* what I did, it worked. Oh, there was a lot of hassle first – the police, the courtroom, all that – but in the end they sent me here, where people listen. It's no picnic in this place – it *is* a sort of prison after all, but at least people listen. People like *you*. Oh, I know you don't believe there was ever a bottle, but you will. I'll *make* you believe when I have all the evidence.

We're gathering evidence, see? Me and Grandma. You know she came to visit last week? Well, that was because she had news for me. She had the cabinet looked at by an expert. The cabinet in the attic. Turns out it's an apothecary's cabinet from the Victorian era. Don't you see – it's exactly the sort of cabinet a *doctor* might have had in those days. Doctor Jekyll, for example.

I can see you smiling. Not with your mouth,

though. Oh no, that wouldn't do at all, would it? Humour the patient – that's the rule, isn't it? Well, listen.

Grandma went to her solicitor, right? He's got the deeds to her house. She looked back to see who'd owned it, and guess what? A *doctor* had it in the eighteen-seventies! *That* was a turn-up if you like, but Grandma was disappointed because his name wasn't Jekyll. Kelly was his name. Joseph Kelly. Anyway she went off to the library in Wexham and did some digging, and it turns out this doctor Kelly died in the house – from *poison*! That gave Grandma quite a turn, I can tell you. Pity the *name*'s wrong, she said. But you see, if you take the J from Joseph and K-E-L-L-Y and jumble them up, you get Jekyll. Try it.

Now, it's well-known that writers sometimes use *real* people in their stories, but they change the names. Well – what if Robert Louis Stevenson based his book on a *true* story – the story of Joseph Kelly? He'd change the name, wouldn't he, and what better way to do that than jumble up the letters? That way, those in the know would spot the trick and the rest would be none the wiser.

Ha – I'm glad to see *that's* got you scribbling.

I want to be believed, because I'm telling the

truth and because I want to go home. I'm not crazy, and I'm certainly not crazy about this place. Like I said, it's a sort of prison. The kids here are weird, and I share a room with five of them. Some of them scream at night. I do myself, but not as often as I did, so maybe the therapy's working.

Anyway I've told you everything. It's up to you whether you believe it or not. I can't *make* you.

What I'd *like* to do, is say to every kid in the world, don't mess with stuff that comes in bottles, or everybody you care about'll leave you and you'll end up in the middle of nowhere like me, making baskets.